The
Stonehenge
Letters

Also by Harry Karlinsky

The Evolution of Inanimate Objects
The Life and Collected Works of Thomas Darwin
(1857–1879)

The Stonehenge Letters

a novel

Harry Karlinsky

Coach House Books, Toronto

First North American edition (published simultaneously with the U.K. edition, from The Friday Project, a division of Harper Collins)

Published with the generous assistance of the Canada Council for the Arts and the Ontario Arts Council. Coach House Books also gratefully acknowledges the support of the Government of Canada through the Canada Book Fund and the Government of Ontario through the Ontario Book Publishing Tax Credit.

This novel is a work of the imagination, although it does incorporate some factual material. We leave it to the reader to to determine which elements are indeed verifiably true.

Library and Archives Canada Cataloguing in Publication

Karlinsky, Harry, 1954-, author
The Stonehenge letters / Harry Karlinsky.

Includes bibliographical references.
Issued in print and electronic formats.
ISBN 978-1-55245-294-3 (pbk.).

I. Title.

PS8621.A6227S76 2014   C813.'6   C2013-907688-3

The Stonehenge Letters is available as an ebook: ISBN 978-1-77056-383-4

Trilithons B and C from the southwest,
Stonehenge, c. 1867.

For Minnie and Will

*They look upon me as pretty much of a monomaniac,
while I have the distinct feeling that I have touched
upon one of the great secrets of nature.*

Sigmund Freud, Letter to Wilhelm Fliess,
21 May 1894

CONTENTS

THE KNÄPPSKALLE FILE

As a (now retired) psychiatrist and amateur historian, I had long been vexed that the clearly deserving Sigmund Freud (1856–1939) had never received the Nobel Prize. In my younger years I had attempted to uncover the reason for this remarkable omission by contacting the Nobel Foundation in Stockholm, the overarching body responsible for the administration of the Nobel Prizes. I was politely but firmly informed that, according to the foundation's statutory rules, 'Proposals received for the award of a prize, and investigations and opinions concerning the award of a prize, may not be divulged.' This stipulation meant that neither the names of those nominated for a Nobel Prize nor the subsequent prize deliberations were made known to the public. As it was more patiently explained to me, the Nobel Foundation could not and would not confirm whether Freud had ever been under consideration for the prize, let alone release the adjudicative details of his evaluation had he ever been nominated.

I was disappointed but not deterred. Though the official channels were closed, the secrecy of the Nobel Prize selection process was not impenetrable. With time and the energy of youth, I was able to glean references to Freud and the Nobel Prize from a large number of unofficial sources. These included the personal diaries of his nominators as well as the private and public correspondence of those who lobbied on Freud's behalf. By my count, Freud had been proposed for the Nobel Prize in Medicine thirty-three separate times between the years 1915 and 1938, once achieving fourteen nominations in the year 1937. It was outrageous that Freud had been overlooked for a Nobel Prize on so many occasions. Yet, despite assertively contacting the Nobel Foundation again and again, I could elicit no explanation for this shameful state of affairs.

In 1974, however, the Swedish government's introduction of new freedom of information legislation had an unintended consequence, one that would dramatically affect the outcome, and direction, of my enquiries. Recipients of the Nobel Prizes in Literature, Physics, Chemistry and the Economic Sciences were then, as now, decided by the Swedish Academy and the Royal Swedish Academy of Sciences, both *private* institutions.[1] In contrast, it was a *publicly* funded medical university – Sweden's Karolinska Institute (*Institutet*, in Swedish) – that determined who received the Nobel Prize in Medicine. As the new legislation afforded access to documents retained in *public* institutions, the secrecy of the Karolinska Institute's prize deliberations was now in jeopardy. The Karolinska Institute manoeuvred quickly. A new *private* body was created and tasked by the faculty of the Karolinska Institute to bestow its prize, thereby preserving the secrecy of its selection.

---

1. Although generally referred to as the Nobel Prize in Economic Sciences and the Nobel Prize in Medicine, the correct designations are the Sveriges Riksbank Prize in Economic Sciences in Memory of Alfred Nobel and the Nobel Prize in Physiology or Medicine, respectively. Note that the Norwegian Nobel Committee awards the Nobel Peace Prize.

These crude shenanigans to circumvent freedom of information did not go unnoticed. The Swedish government immediately demanded that the secrecy surrounding the awarding of all the Nobel Prizes be lifted. After contentious negotiations, a key conciliatory revision within the statutes of the Nobel Foundation emerged as follows:

A prize-awarding body may, however, after due consideration in each individual case, permit access to material which formed the basis for the evaluation and decision concerning a prize, for purposes of research in intellectual history. Such permission may not, however, be granted until at least fifty years have elapsed after the date on which the decision in question was made.

I was delighted. With access to the Nobel Archives now available, I was determined to learn the real truth, sordid or otherwise, behind Freud's lengthy series of disappointments.

After years of inadvertent delay for both professional and personal reasons,[2] I at last arrived in Stockholm in the spring of 2013 to conduct my research. The twenty-nine-letter Swedish alphabet was an immediate and unexpected challenge; fortunately, undergraduate students from Stockholm University were available to translate documents at a reasonable ten Swedish kronor per page. The greater obstacle, however, lay with the quality of available records, which fell into four groupings: letters of nomination, reports on candidates, minutes of the working committees and minutes of the larger voting assemblies. It was the nature of the material

---

2. Although I was never hesitant to use self-disclosure as a therapeutic tool in my psychiatric practice, my protective editors have insisted I minimize my lifelong battle with hypochondriasis in this account (but see Appendix II).

in the latter two categories that was most limiting. Instead of unearthing detailed and candid discussions of the relative merits of Freud's work as I had envisioned, only tallies of votes and final decisions were recorded.

I abandoned the effort altogether when an obliging student, aware of my interest, drew my attention to an obscure article by a Swedish psychiatrist, Dr. Carl-Magnus Stolt, titled 'Why Did Freud Never Receive the Nobel Prize?' Stolt had already reviewed the relevant archival material, leaving no doubt as to either the priority or the thoroughness of his findings. In brief, Freud's candidacy was based on those accomplishments one would expect to be cited: his courageous new insights concerning the unconscious, the significance of dreams and the stages of infantile sexuality; his development of such novel concepts as the id, the ego and the superego; and perhaps, most importantly, his introduction of psychoanalysis. As a number of his nominators stressed, Freud's so-called 'talking cure' was the first effective treatment for a range of psychological disorders, including hysteria and the sexual perversions.

Yet Freud's repeated rejections were not for the reasons I had suspected. Stolt found no indication that either anti-Semitism or the personal animosity of members on the Nobel Committee had undermined Freud's chances. There was also no evidence that political considerations had constituted a factor, such as the fear that Freud's selection in the 1930s might incite Nazi Germany. Instead, Freud's work – at least as judged in the official documents – was viewed as too subjective for traditional scientific evaluation. In a cruel twist, one of the most damaging observations used against Freud was that he was also aggressively

Figure 1. Sigmund Freud.

promoted for the Nobel Prize in Literature, once earning an official nomination from the French author and Nobel Laureate Romain Rolland. The flattering appraisal that Freud's case studies lent themselves well to the conventions of fiction undermined any perception of Freud as an objective physician–scientist.

Disheartened, I considered other lines of investigation. As Freud had never encountered or written about Alfred Nobel (the man whose fortune was used after his death to finance the Nobel Prizes), I first distracted myself by reconstructing Nobel's emotional life by way of Freud's psychological principles. Once this small exercise was completed (see Appendix I), I then sought to clarify whether any psychiatrist had ever been awarded the Nobel Prize in Medicine. There were two: the first was Julius Wagner-Jauregg who, in 1927, earned the prize for his discovery that malaria inoculation could be effective in the treatment of neurosyphilis, at that time an incurable disease.[3] The second psychiatrist-laureate was Eric R. Kandel, a co-winner in 2000 for delineating the physiological basis of neuronal memory. Neither of these individuals nor their respective areas of research were of particular interest. Nor were the

---

3. The curative factor was the high fever associated with malaria, an illness normally transmitted to humans by the bite of the *Anopheles* mosquito. In his earliest experiment, Wagner-Jauregg deliberately exposed a psychiatric in-patient ward to swarms of infected mosquitoes. These (the mosquitoes) were difficult to contain and quickly spread malaria throughout the entire hospital. After a significant number of staff and patients contracted a malignant type of malaria and died, Wagner-Jauregg discontinued his investigations. Years later when the research was reinstituted (at another setting), Wagner-Jauregg now knew to withdraw infected blood from patients already ill with malaria. He then used this infected blood to inoculate patients afflicted with neurosyphilis, most of whom developed attacks of fever, and some of whom were cured.

brutal surgeries of António Egas Moniz, a Portuguese neurologist often incorrectly assumed to be a psychiatrist. Moniz won a 1949 Nobel Prize in Medicine for developing the now-discredited leucotomy (or 'lobotomy'), a barbaric surgical procedure that he recklessly inflicted upon psychotic patients. Ironically, Moniz would have made a far more legitimate Nobel Laureate for his pioneering radiological investigations of the carotid arteries and other vasculature, work for which he also received Nobel nominations.[4]

For a period of time, I attempted to compile a list of Nobel Laureates who had been analyzed by Freud. Although I failed to uncover any such individuals within Freud's relatively small circle of patients, I had more success identifying those Nobelists treated within the wider psychoanalytic community. Saul Bellow, winner of the Nobel Prize in Literature in 1976, was especially indebted to Freud's disciples. Analyzed by at least four well-known therapists, Bellow once shared his apartment with an Orgone Accumulator, a large zinc-lined rectangular crate roughly the size of a small outhouse. The contraption, invented by the controversial psychoanalyst Wilhelm Reich, ostensibly 'accumulated' orgone, an allegedly ubiquitous life force supposed essential for sexual vitality. Bellow was reported to have retreated into his Orgone Accumulator for hours, most often to read, but periodically to gag himself with a handkerchief and then unabashedly scream out for sexual release.

---

4. Moniz was shot eight times by one of his paranoid patients at the beginning of World War II, but survived wounds to his right hand and torso. Despite speculation within the psychiatric community, it remains uncertain whether Moniz lobotomized the assailant either before or, more likely, after the assault. Although Moniz slowly recovered, he gradually withdrew from medical practice and retired in 1944.

I was also aware, of course, of the profoundly disturbed nightmares of Wolfgang Pauli, winner of the Nobel Prize in Physics in 1945. These so interested the Swiss psychoanalyst Carl Jung that he published interpretations of four hundred of Pauli's dreams and visions in what became the twelfth volume of Jung's *Collected Works*.[5] Jung and an apparently healthier Pauli subsequently collaborated on the subject of 'synchronicity': unrelated events that occurred together as 'meaningful coincidences.' The resulting work was a completely mad fusion of quantum mechanics and parapsychology.

I was soon able to accumulate the names of more than forty other laureates who, like Bellow and Pauli, had benefited substantially from psychoanalysis. Again, however, I discontinued my enquiries, this time on re-examining my motives and recognizing my real agenda: a childish means of highlighting Freud's disgraceful oversight by the various Nobel Prize selection committees. In truth, it was more personal than that. Fifty-five years ago, I was inspired by Freud's writings to choose psychiatry as my profession. For forty-five years, I practised psychotherapy utilizing Freud's principles. As I approached retirement, I was uncomfortably aware that Freud was no longer venerated in the psychiatric community and that the prestige of psychoanalysis as a discipline was in rapid decline. Indeed, there were 'biological' psychiatrists who dismissed Freud's theories as the unverifiable beliefs of a man bordering on madness. More than once I had to defend the nature of my work to the (much younger) Chair of my Department. In now

5. Jung was nominated only once for the Nobel Prize in Medicine (in 1950). Compare this to Freud's thirty-three nominations.

numerating and restating Freud's accomplishments, and re-examining his Nobel defeats, it was obvious I was also attempting to legitimize my own career in the process.

I was in the midst of these private musings, when – browsing aimlessly in the Nobel Archives – I stumbled upon the 'Crackpot' file, the source of the remarkable story that follows. Nominations for each Nobel Prize are intended to be elicited only by invitation. Each year, the various Nobel Prize Committees invite, in confidence, thousands of qualified individuals, including all previous Nobel Laureates, to nominate deserving candidates other than themselves. Those names proposed by invited nominators – the 'official' nominees – are then considered for the coming year's Nobel Prizes. Despite well-publicized admonitions that only official nominations are adjudicated, the Nobel Prize Committees still receive a substantial number of unsolicited applications, many from individuals who nominate themselves on the basis of questionable achievements. These unsought applications are immediately consigned to the B file, or the *Knäppskalle* ('Crackpot') file as the committee members more affectionately know it, and are rife with such claims as well-intentioned but ill-conceived cures for cancer and flawed designs for perpetual-motion machines. The file made for sad but compelling reading and I began to spend more time perusing its contents.

It soon became evident, to a psychiatrist at least, that a significant proportion of those who nominated themselves were in the throes of serious psychiatric illness. Untreated mania, with its pathognomonic features of inflated self-esteem and irrepressible self-confidence, was pervasive. Euphoric applicants, without any prior training or demonstrated expertise, were pronouncing definitively on such matters as pandemics and elementary particle physics or declaring lengthy and incoherent memoirs as great works of literature. Of more concern were those applications fuelled by the bizarre delusions of individuals with psychotic disorders. The frequency of such submissions suggested that there might be merit in conducting a formal review of all unsolicited applications in an attempt to establish the underlying prevalence of psychopathology. Perhaps the resulting data might also identify a unique cluster of symptoms precipitated by the siren song of a Nobel Prize.

As the *Knäppskalle* file was organized by year of application, I began in 1901, the first year in which the Nobel Prizes were awarded. The number of entries on file increased substantially each year and it was difficult not to be impressed by the range and power of the human imagination, diseased or otherwise. One submission in particular caught my attention. Handwritten in Russian, it contained three unusual figures, two of which related to earthworms. The third, torn from a text written in English, was a sketch depicting 'one of the fallen Druidical stones at Stonehenge.' Intrigued, I requested the assistance of a translator. In brief, the submission's central thesis was that a causal relationship existed between the digestive habits of earthworms and why the enormous stone pillars at Stonehenge were gradually sinking into the ground. Despite its unusual supposition, it was a serious account and appeared to have been written as a focused response to an enquiry from a Mr. Sohlman.

By this stage in my research, I was able to recognize Sohlman's name as that of the principal executor of Alfred Nobel's will and, for many years, the executive director of the Nobel Foundation. To my surprise, I also recognized the applicant's name: Ivan Pavlov, winner of the 1904 Nobel Prize in Medicine. Although I had not been exposed to Pavlov's work on classical conditioning since the early years of my psychiatric training, the submission's arguments and style of writing seemed consistent with Pavlov's well-known reputation for meticulous observation and measurement. Perplexed, I continued my review of the *Knäppskalle* file, utilizing translators as required, until it was complete.

In the end, five other letters related to Stonehenge were addressed to Mr. Ragnar Sohlman. Remarkably, early Nobel Laureates had written all but one. Even more remarkably, all alluded to solving the 'mystery' of Stonehenge.

And so began my journey of discovery, from Ivan Pavlov to Theodore Roosevelt to Rudyard Kipling to Marie Curie to Albert Einstein to a gentleman by the name of Norman Lockyer.

Or, as Freud once said more eloquently, 'From error to error, one discovers the entire truth.'

PART ONE

ALFRED NOBEL'S
LAST WILL AND TESTAMENT

CHAPTER I

ALFRED NOBEL

For those readers unfamiliar with the early history of the
Nobel Prizes, the man in whose honour they were named
– Alfred Bernhard Nobel – was born in Stockholm, Sweden,
in 1833. The third eldest of four sons (two younger siblings
died in infancy), Alfred's childhood years in Sweden were
spent in relative poverty. His father, Immanuel Nobel, a self-
taught pioneer in the arms industry, had been forced into
bankruptcy the year of Alfred's birth. Immanuel subsequently
left his wife Andriette and their children in Sweden to pursue
opportunities, first in Finland and later in Russia, that would
re-establish the family's wealth. It was not until 1842 that
the Nobel family was reunited in St. Petersburg. By then,
Immanuel had convinced Tsar Nicholas I that submerged
wooden barrels filled with gunpowder were an effective
means to protect Russia's coastal cities from enemy naval
attack. This was surprising, as virtually all of Immanuel's
brightly painted underwater mines failed to detonate, even
those brought ashore and struck severely with hammers.

Due to the ongoing military tensions that eventually
led to Russia's involvement in the Crimean War (1853–
1856), Immanuel's munitions factory prospered and Alfred's
adolescent years in St. Petersburg were privileged. With
the assistance of private tutors, he became fluent in five

languages and excelled in both the sciences and the arts. At age seventeen, Alfred was sent abroad for two years in order to train as a chemical engineer. In Paris, his principal destination, he was introduced to Ascanio Sobrero, the first chemist to successfully produce nitroglycerine. On Alfred's return to St. Petersburg in 1852, he and his father began to experiment with the highly explosive liquid, initially considered too volatile to be of commercial value.

Despite initial setbacks, Alfred Nobel quickly established himself as a talented chemist and aggressive entrepreneur. His most important discoveries – the detonator, dynamite and blasting gelatin – would form the lucrative underpinnings of an industrial empire. By the time of his death in 1896, Nobel held 355 patents and owned explosives manufacturing plants and laboratories in more than twenty countries. According to his executors, his net assets amounted to over 31 million Swedish kronor, the current equivalent of 265 million American dollars.

As his legacy, Nobel directed in his will that his immense fortune be used to establish a series of prizes. These were to be annual awards for exceptional contributions in the fields of physics, chemistry, physiology or medicine, literature and peace. The will then ended with a curious closing directive:

> *Finally, it is my express wish that following my death my veins shall be opened, and when this has been done and competent Doctors have confirmed clear signs of death, my remains shall be cremated in a so-called crematorium.*

It was Freud who stated that there was no better document than the will to reveal the character of its writer. Nobel was terrified of being buried alive, a phobia termed taphophobia (from the Greek *taphos*, for 'grave'). The triggering stimulus, at least as cited in Nobel's conventional biographies, was Verdi's opera *Aida*. Nobel had attended its European premiere at La Scala, Milan, on 8 February 1872 and was deeply affected by the closing scene. Aida, a slave in Egypt (but, in truth, an Ethiopian princess), chooses to join her condemned lover Radamès as he is about to be sealed within a tomb. Horrified by the imagery of their impending immurement, Nobel immediately developed a deep-rooted fear that he, too, was destined to die while sentient and trapped. To address his anxiety, Nobel first carried a crowbar on his person. He next relied on a 'life-signalling' coffin of his own design.[6] In the end, Nobel trusted on the certainty of cremation. It was only on realizing he was now at risk for being *burned* alive, as opposed to *buried* alive, that a cautious Nobel also stipulated that his 'veins shall be opened' prior to his cremation (i.e., exsanguination by way of phlebotomy).

Years later, Nobel was to die suddenly in San Remo, Italy. As his will, the provisions of which were unknown to others, was on deposit in a private Swedish bank, it took three days before his executors learned of his morbid last wishes. By then, Nobel's corpse had been embalmed, a standard funerary practice in Italy during the 1890s and a

---

6. This was based on a prototype developed by Nobel's father. The device was equipped with air and feeding tubes, an escape hatch, and various methods to communicate with those above ground. On learning that others also feared premature burial, Nobel patented his invention and anticipated significant sales. To promote his 'life-signalling' coffin, Nobel staged dramatic publicity stunts in which willing members of the public were fed beer and sausages while interred underground. It was after one such demonstration, in which a volunteer almost suffocated to death, that Nobel prudently reconsidered the viability of the entire enterprise.

Figure 2. The Nobel Family. Immanuel Nobel (top left), Andriette Nobel (top right) and the Nobel brothers: Robert, Alfred, Ludvig and baby Emil (bottom, clockwise from top).

process that, by good fortune, begins with bleeding the veins of the deceased.

Sadly, even Nobel had recognized he was troubled throughout his life by more than an operatic death scene. Though capable of congenial social interactions and outright levity in the right company, Nobel had lived a lonely existence without a lifelong partner or children. It was a lament he would frequently share, even in letters to strangers, as evidenced by the following admission:

> *At the age of fifty-four, when one is completely alone in the world, and shown consideration by nobody except a paid servant, one's thoughts become gloomy indeed.*

With bitter insight, Nobel accepted his unwanted isolation as central to his melancholic outlook and the frequent episodes of depression that were particularly prevalent in his middle years. Nobel would refer to these periods of despair as visits from the 'spirits of *Niflheim*,' the cold and misty afterworld in Nordic mythology and the location of *Hel*, to where those who failed to die a heroic death were banished.

Remarkably, Nobel failed to consider the root cause of his isolation, which was directly attributable to the loss of the many family members and colleagues who had died sudden violent deaths (i.e., were blown to smithereens) as a result of their association with him. In 1856, the Crimean War had ended unfavourably for Russia, in no small part due to the failure of Immanuel's ineffectual mines to cut off crucial enemy shipping lanes in the Baltic Sea. The financial circumstances of the Nobel family declined accordingly. After retreating hastily to Stockholm with only limited resources, Alfred and his father continued their experiments with nitroglycerine. On 3 September 1864, five individuals died in a horrific explosion; among the casualties was Emil Nobel, Alfred's younger brother. To compound the tragedy, a grieving Immanuel suffered a debilitating stroke just one month later. Yet within two months of Emil's death, Alfred was defiantly exporting the world's first source of industrial-grade nitroglycerine. Due to the concerns of government officials about the dangers of the unstable compound, its preparation was restricted to a barge anchored on a lake located beyond Stockholm's city limits. Despite such safety measures, a distressing loss of lives would continue to accompany the commercial production of nitroglycerine, which Nobel quickly extended by establishing factories throughout Europe. Although Nobel refused to express remorse in public (possibly on the advice of his lawyers), the deaths of so many of his employees and innocent bystanders would have a lingering impact on his sensitive disposition.[7]

Nobel's poor physical health would also constantly undermine his fragile temperament. As a delicate and sickly child, Nobel frequented health spas while still in his late teens. Troubled by chronic indigestion, he was once diagnosed with scurvy, and for a period of months consumed only horseradish and grape juice. In his late forties, Nobel developed severe migraine headaches, and then, more seriously, the onset of paroxysmal spasms of chest pain. Though the latter symptoms were initially assumed to be hysterical in nature, he was eventually diagnosed as suffering from a debilitating form of angina pectoris. As he aged, his attacks

---

7. It was Freud who first warned other therapists that an unconscious sense of guilt was 'the most powerful of all obstacles to recovery.'

Figure 3. Alfred Nobel.

worsened. While visiting Paris in October 1896, Nobel had a particularly severe episode. As he drolly wrote,

Isn't it the irony of fate that I have been prescribed nitro-glycerine to be taken internally! They call it Trinitrin, so as not to scare the chemist and the public.[8]

Within two months of returning to his winter residence in San Remo, Italy, Nobel suffered a catastrophic cerebral hemorrhage. On 10 December 1896, agitated, semi-paralyzed and attended only by Italian servants unable to comprehend his last words, which were uttered in Swedish, Nobel died as he had feared, trapped within his body, frightened and alone.

---

8. Dr William Murrell, a British physician, first discovered the therapeutic effects of extremely small doses of nitroglycerine for angina pectoris in the late 1870s.

CHAPTER 2

LILLJEQVIST AND SOHLMAN

The challenge of implementing Nobel's will fell to his two designated executors.

As Executors of my testamentary dispositions, I hereby appoint Mr. Ragnar Sohlman, resident at Bofors, Värmland, and Mr. Rudolf Lilljequist, 31 Malmskill- nadsgatan, Stockholm, and at Bengtsfors near Udde- valla. To compensate for their pains and attention, I grant to Mr. Ragnar Sohlman, who will presumably have to devote most time to this matter, One Hundred Thousand Crowns, and to Mr. Rudolf Lilljequist, Fifty Thousand Crowns.

Nobel had only recently met Rudolf Lilljeqvist, a Swedish civil engineer, in May of 1895. Their initial discussions had revolved around the electrolytic decomposition of salt. Nobel and Lilljeqvist developed an instant rapport, likely due to a shared antipathy toward lawyers.[9] Years of litigation involving alleged patent infringements, charges of industrial espionage and a series of wrongful death

---

9. Nobel's and Lilljeqvist's distaste for lawyers was most explicitly expressed in the form of the derogatory jokes they shared, often to the effect that lawyers were akin to 'red-taped parasites.' Freud, whose works included his 1905 book *The Joke and Its Relation to the Unconscious*, recognized such acerbic humour as an adaptive defence mechanism, a cleansing catharsis and a conduit to camaraderie.

lawsuits had left Nobel with a fierce aversion to those in the legal profession. Lilljeqvist was equally wary, a victim of incompetent lawyers who had undermined his previous efforts to court potential investors. After only three months of congenial negotiations, conducted without legal advice, Nobel agreed to fund Lilljeqvist's proposal to establish an electrochemical plant in Bengtsfors, a village in north-west Sweden. Nobel had obviously been deeply impressed with Lilljeqvist, and despite their brief acquaintance, had developed an immediate confidence in his new partner's acumen and ethical principles.

Although Lilljeqvist subsequently declined Nobel's invitation to take up a well-paid managerial position at a weapons foundry (AB Bofors, see p. 40), the two men engaged in a second collaboration just prior to Nobel's death. The impetus was the unpredictable and explosive nature of nitroglycerine at temperatures higher than 180 degrees Celsius. As the chemical production of nitroglycerine created heat, the temperature of the nitration vats within Nobel's factories required careful monitoring. In practical terms, this meant that one employee was assigned the task of staring at a thermometer throughout the production process. Not surprisingly, the hypnotic nature of the activity frequently induced sleep, and lethal gaffes were prevalent.

In an effort to reduce fatalities, Nobel had first mandated that the relevant workers must complete their shifts without shoes and wearing only a single sock. The principle was simple: Nobel knew from the privations of his early childhood that it was impossible to fall asleep if one foot was colder than the other. It was only upon learning that this prescription contravened nascent employee

Figure 4. Rudolf Lilljeqvist.

safety regulations that Nobel rescinded the directive. To gain a first-hand impression of the inherent challenge, Nobel then joined his own labour force. Struggling to stay alert during one shift, an exhausted Nobel realized that it would require a high degree of wakefulness for a worker to remain upright while seated on an unstable surface; should a worker still manage to fall asleep, there would be an obligatory tumble and abrupt arousal. Nobel subsequently conceived of the exact solution – the one-legged stool – while enduring the last act of Wagner's *Die Meistersinger von Nürnberg*. Nobel patented his invention and Lilljeqvist undertook its manufacture. Despite worker protests, the one-legged wooden stool became an immediate and effective industry standard.[10]

The other executor appointed in Nobel's will was Ragnar Sohlman. In contrast to his purely professional relationship with Lilljeqvist, Nobel's association with Sohlman was more personal. Sohlman, a Swedish-born chemical engineer like Nobel, was only twenty-five years old at the time of Nobel's death. The two men had first met three years earlier. In 1893, Sohlman had moved to Paris to begin work as Nobel's personal assistant. After efficiently reorganizing Nobel's reference library and his extensive files, Sohlman was precipitously transferred to Nobel's new laboratory in San Remo, Italy. Sohlman had little choice but to move: the French government had accused Nobel of stealing a

---

10. Freud had resolved a similar dilemma years earlier while working as a house officer at the General Hospital of Vienna. It had come to his attention that the nursing staff and orderlies were consistently falling asleep during their overnight shifts. To rectify the matter, Freud prescribed the invigorating effects of cocaine. Unlike the labour resistance Nobel encountered, Freud was hailed as a local champion (Freud, 'Über Coca. Centralblatt für die ges,' 1885).

Figure 5. A one-legged stool.

formula from a French competitor and had forcibly closed his laboratory on the outskirts of Paris.

Sohlman's tenure at San Remo was brief. Within a year of his arrival, Nobel acquired controlling interest in AB Bofors, a large Swedish ironworks and weapons foundry located on the outskirts of Karlskoga, a town in western Sweden. As part of the purchase price, Nobel also acquired ownership of Björkborn Manor, a comfortable but slightly worn residence on the grounds of the property. With the assistance of his nephew Hjalmer, Nobel planned to refurbish the manor as his permanent home. After years of an unsettled and itinerant lifestyle, Nobel had finally grown nostalgic for the country of his birth and had resolved to spend his remaining years in Sweden.

Both Nobel and Sohlman moved from San Remo to Karlskoga in early 1895. Sohlman had, by then, favourably married. With Nobel's permission, he had taken a short holiday the preceding year to pursue his courtship of Ragnhild Strom, a Norwegian woman he had met through family friends. Once living in Karlskoga, the young couple began to dine with Nobel, an arrangement then unusual in an employer–employee relationship. Soon, Nobel was inviting Sohlman to address him as Father.[11] Though Sohlman was too embarrassed to do so, he did begin to greet Nobel by his Christian name and to refer to himself as 'your affectionate friend R' when signing his letters to Nobel.

Nobel's tender feelings for Sohlman would prove lifesaving. In the early 1890s, Salomon August Andrée, Sweden's first balloonist, had roused patriotic fervour by

11. Nobel demonstrated other unusual behaviours. See Appendix I for a complete (alphabetized) list of Nobel's dominant personality traits, defence mechanisms and primary mental disorders.

Figure 6. Ragnar Sohlman.

proposing to pilot a balloon to the North Pole in order to claim the iconic destination in the name of Sweden. Anticipating the arrival of aerial warfare, Nobel envisioned that manned balloons might one day become effective vehicles to drop bombs on enemy positions. Eager to participate in all aspects of the explosives industry, Nobel became one of Andrée's earliest and most generous financial backers.

In the summer of 1896, Andrée visited Bofors at Nobel's invitation. During the ensuing discussions, in which Sohlman also participated, Nobel encouraged Andrée to persevere with his dream of Arctic sovereignty. Earlier that spring, Andrée's first attempt to launch his balloon had failed, and there were critics who now viewed the entire notion as foolhardy. Nobel's optimism, however, was infectious and a re-energized Andrée assured Nobel he would re-attempt the flight in the coming year. As Andrée's large hydrogen balloon required a three-man crew, Sohlman volunteered – unexpectedly – to join the proposed expedition. The following day Nobel, concerned for Sohlman's safety, spoke to Andrée privately and threatened to withdraw his financial support should the flight proceed with Sohlman on board. Andrée duly informed Sohlman that, in light of Sohlman's meteorological inexperience, his participation would no longer be possible on what would ultimately prove to be a doomed expedition.[12]

12. On 11 July 1897, Andrée and two younger colleagues, Nils Strindberg and Knut Frænkel, lifted off from Danes Island, part of the Svalbard archipelago, a group of islands located off Norway's northernmost coast. After less than three days aloft, the balloon crashed on pack ice, having travelled approximately three hundred miles but still far short of the North Pole. Though unhurt, the three men were hopelessly unprepared to survive the severe Arctic conditions. One of their first mistakes was to immediately shoot and eat the homing pigeons on board. These had been intended to convey messages to the outside world and had been

Figure 7. S. A. Andrée's doomed Arctic balloon
expedition (1897).

Nobel summered at Björkborn Manor in 1895 and 1896. Although he had initially intended to live year-round within its poorly insulated quarters, Nobel found he could no longer endure the bitterly cold Swedish winters. To avoid the inhospitable weather, he would stay instead at his Italian residence in San Remo. On 7 December 1896, in a letter mailed from Villa San Remo, Nobel would write his last words to Sohlman:

> *Alas, my health is so poor again that I can only scribble these words with difficulty. But I shall come back as soon as possible to the subjects which interest us both,*
>
> *Affectionately, Alfred Nobel*

One day later, Nobel collapsed into a state of semi-consciousness. Although Sohlman was alerted of Nobel's abrupt deterioration and immediately left Sweden for Italy, he did not arrive until shortly after Nobel's death. It was there, while assisting with Nobel's funeral arrangements, that Sohlman first learned of the provisions of Nobel's will and his unexpected responsibilities. When Lilljeqvist was informed by telegram one day later that he was also an executor of Nobel's testamentary dispositions, he was as surprised as Sohlman.

---

trained to return to their base in northern Norway. Pulling sledges on foot and inching slowly southward on ice floes, the men survived for over three months, living largely on a diet of raw polar bear meat. It was not until 1930 that the crew of a Norwegian sealing expedition found remains of the final camp on Kvitøya, an isolated and deserted island. One of the preserved artefacts was a waterlogged tin box that contained Nils Strindberg's photographic film. Ninety-three prints were salvaged, a remarkable and touching visual record of the men's ill-fated journey.

CHAPTER 3

NOBEL'S LAST WILL AND TESTAMENT

Nobel's Last Will and Testament was dated 27 November 1895. An unexpectedly informal document, the will was handwritten in Swedish and signed by four Swedish witnesses at the Swedish–Norwegian Club in Paris in early December 1895. After specifying individual bequests to eighteen family members, servants and acquaintances, the will read as follows:

> *The whole of my remaining realizable estate shall be dealt with in the following way: the capital, invested in safe securities by my executors, shall constitute a fund, the interest on which shall be annually distributed in the form of prizes to those who, during the preceding year, shall have conferred the greatest benefit to mankind. The said interest shall be divided into five equal parts, which shall be apportioned as follows: one part to the person who shall have made the most important discovery or invention within the field of physics; one part to the person who shall have made the most important chemical discovery or improvement; one part to the person who shall have made the most important discovery within the domain of physiology or medicine; one part to the person who shall have produced in the field of literature the most outstanding work in an ideal*

direction; and one part to the person who shall have done the most or the best work for fraternity between nations, for the abolition or reduction of standing armies and for the holding and promotion of peace congresses. The prize for physics and chemistry shall be awarded by the Swedish Academy of Sciences; that for physiological or medical works by Karolinska Institutet in Stockholm; that for literature by the Academy in Stockholm; and that for champions of peace by a committee of five persons to be elected by the Norwegian Storting. It is my express wish that in awarding the prizes no consideration whatever shall be given to the nationality of the candidates, but that the most worthy shall receive the prize, whether he be a Scandinavian or not.

It was a remarkable philanthropic vision. As Sohlman and Lilljeqvist immediately recognized, however, the will – stubbornly constructed by Nobel without legal advice – contained significant deficiencies that might easily undermine its realization. For assistance, the two executors turned to Carl Lindhagen, a young lawyer who would later serve a long tenure as Chief Magistrate of Stockholm. The three men quickly established that Sohlman, despite substantial reservations on his part, would take on the role of principal executor. Lilljeqvist would be available to provide advice and encouragement, but his new business interests in Bengtsfors would preclude more active involvement. Lindhagen would serve as legal counsel.[13]

As Lindhagen predicted, the successful execution of the will would require resolution of three contentious issues.

13. Despite Lilljeqvist's off-putting lawyer jokes, the three men worked well together.

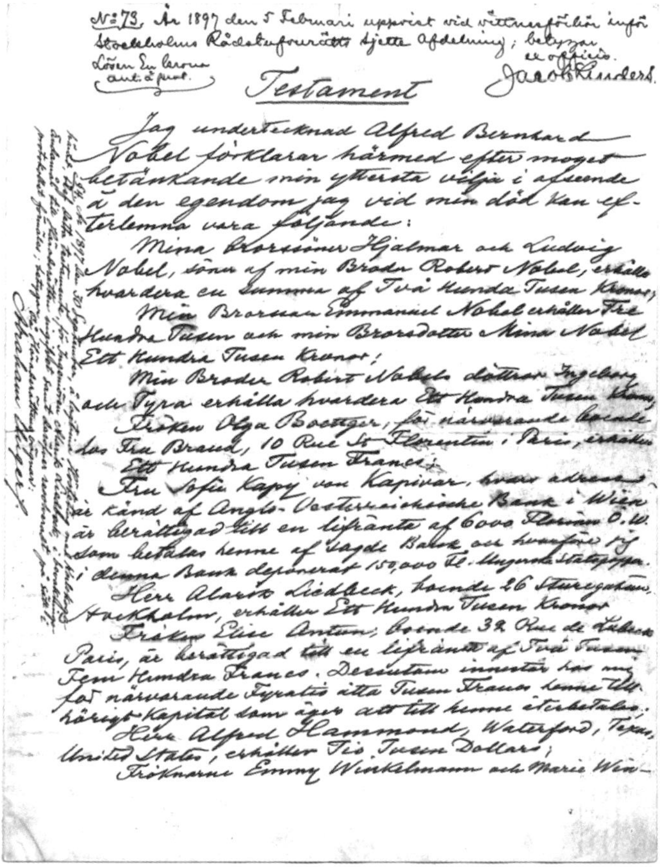
N:o 73. År 1897 den 5 Februari uppvist vid vittnesförhör inför Stockholms Rådstufvurätts Sjette Afdelning; betygar ex officio.
Jacob Sanders.
Lösen En krona ant. å prot.

Testament

Jag undertecknad Alfred Bernhard Nobel förklarar härmed efter moget betänkande min yttersta vilja i afseende å den egendom jag vid min död kan efterlemna vara följande:

Mina brorssöner Hjalmar och Ludvig Nobel, söner af min Broder Robert Nobel, erhålla hvardera en summa af Två Hundra Tusen Kronor;

Min Brorson Emmanuel Nobel erhåller Tre Hundra Tusen och min Brorsdotter Mina Nobel Ett Hundra Tusen Kronor;

Min Broder Robert Nobels döttrar Ingeborg och Tyra erhålla hvardera Ett Hundra Tusen Kronor;

Fröken Olga Boettger, för närvarande boende hos Fru Brand, 10 Rue St Florentin i Paris, erhåller Ett Hundra Tusen Francs;

Fru Sofie Kapy von Kapivar, hvars adress är känd af Anglo-Oesterreichische Bank i Wien är berättigad till en lifränta af 6000 Florins Ö.W. som betalas henne af sagde Bank och hvarför jag i denna Bank deponerat 150,000 Fl. i Ungerska Statspapper.

Herr Alarik Liedbeck, boende 26 Sturegatan, Stockholm, erhåller Ett Hundra Tusen Kronor;

Fröken Elise Antun, boende 32 Rue de Lubeck, Paris, är berättigad till en lifränta af Två Tusen Fem Hundra Francs. Dessutom innestår hos mig för närvarande Fyratio åtta Tusen Francs henne tillhörigt Kapital som äger att till henne återbetalas.

Herr Alfred Hammond, Waterford, Texas, United States, erhåller Tio Tusen Dollars;

Fröknarne Emmy Winkelmann och Marie Win-

Figure 8. The first page of Alfred Nobel's will.

The most problematic of these involved the legal clarification of Nobel's last permanent residence, his so-called 'true' domicile. This determination would, in turn, establish which court in which country would grant probate. As Nobel's intention had been to live out his years in Björkborn Manor, Lindhagen advised Sohlman and Lilljeqvist to apply for probate in a Swedish court. It was not certain, however, whether Nobel would be declared a resident of Sweden and that, *a fortiori*, a Swedish court would adjudicate the validity and terms of the will. The courts would consider, for example, that Nobel also owned a mansion in Paris and a country home in Italy at the time of his death. Should Paris be determined to have been Nobel's true domicile, as the French authorities immediately requested, the financial consequences would be particularly severe. In addition to the crushing inheritance taxes imposed in France, the legality of the entire will would also be in jeopardy due to the much more stringent laws of the *Code Napoléon*.

A second prickly subject was the immediate opposition of disappointed relatives who bitterly viewed their inheritance as insufficient. To add to the perceived slight, an earlier will that Nobel had rescinded had contained far more generous bequests to individual heirs than the current iteration. Nobel's family was also concerned that the interest-generating capital required to fund the annual prizes appeared to depend on immediately liquidating Nobel's vast financial assets. Selling all investments would jeopardize the financial stability of a number of Nobel family holdings, particularly that of the large Russian oil company started by Nobel's two older brothers.

The third potential impasse was the astonishing fact that Nobel had never discussed with any representatives of the institutions he had named in his will his intention that they administer the prizes he sought to establish. The cooperation of any, let alone all, of these institutional bodies was far from certain. To further embroil matters, the designation of the Norwegian *Storting* (Parliament) to award the peace prize drew a strong political backlash. Nobel had written his will in 1895, at a time when Sweden and Norway were still united as one country. By the end of 1896, the dissolution of their fragile political union was imminent. The inclusion of Norway now bordered on treason, inciting Sweden's reigning King Oscar II to petition Nobel's nephew and most influential heir, Emanuel Nobel, to challenge the will on patriotic grounds. One of the few family members who was a strong advocate for his uncle's wishes, Emanuel was, by the time he received the king's request, defiant:

> *Your Majesty – I will not expose my family to the risk of reproaches in future for having appropriated funds which rightfully belonged to deserving scientists.*

Remarkably, all obstacles were eventually resolved. The courts sided with the executors and the will was favourably probated in Sweden. Thanks to financial concessions and the support of Emanuel Nobel, all branches of the Nobel family eventually agreed to the will's provisions.[14] Each

14. The last holdout was Nobel's nephew Hjalmer, although his objections had little to do with the amount of his inheritance. Nobel had asked Hjalmer to refurbish Björkborn Manor upon his purchase of the dilapidated mansion. As the Manor was situated on the largest area of open land on the Bofors Estate, Nobel had installed a prototype of a 250 mm cannon on its large veranda and created an impromptu firing range. After a prized Orloff stallion strayed into the line of fire, Nobel had its head, once located, stuffed and prominently placed in the Manor's upper hallway. Despite Hjalmer's protests on aesthetic grounds, Nobel refused to remove the 'eyesore' and ill feelings lingered on both sides.

prize-awarding body also came to accept the terms of the will, and collaborated on establishing clearer instructions related to the distribution of the prizes. Nobel's assets were liquidated and a single fund was constituted that would be managed by an entity referred to as the Nobel Foundation. This foundation would also be responsible for overseeing the Nobel Prize ceremonies.

On 29 June 1900, the Swedish government approved the statutes of the Nobel Foundation by royal ordinance. These contained the clarifications related to the wording of the will and such details as the establishment of the prize-awarding Nobel Committees. On 10 December 1901, precisely five years after the death of Alfred Nobel, the first Nobel Prizes were awarded: in physics to Wilhelm Conrad Röntgen, in chemistry to Jacobus H. van 't Hoff, in medicine to Emil von Behring, and in literature to Sully Prudhomme. The Nobel Peace Prize was awarded jointly to Jean Henry Dunant and Frédéric Passy. Each laureate received a diploma, a gold medal and a significant sum of money; later that day, a celebratory banquet was held in their honour at Stockholm's Grand Hôtel. As Ragnar Sohlman so elegantly stated, 'The long struggle over Nobel's will was now at an end.'

It was Freud who said the optimist sees the rose and not its thorns.

PART TWO

AN UNEXPECTED PRIZE

CHAPTER 4

'FRAU SOFIE' AND COUNTESS BERTHA KINSKY

With the establishment of the Nobel Foundation in 1900, Sohlman's responsibilities as principal executor diminished substantially. No longer required to consolidate and administer Nobel's financial assets, Sohlman could finally turn to the systematic organization of Nobel's personal files. These were extensive, as Nobel saved all incoming letters. It was also his habit to travel with a portable hectograph, about the size of a large briefcase. With little effort, Nobel could methodically reproduce onionskin duplicates of all outgoing correspondence, which he then kept in a large number of carelessly organized folders and folio boxes. Most letters were written in Swedish or Russian, but Nobel also corresponded in French, English and German. Sohlman, also a competent multilinguist due to Nobel's influence and the nature of their work together, was surprised (and dismayed) to find that he now faced the challenging task of cataloguing over ten thousand documents.

Regrettably, Sohlman was already familiar with one specific folder that he himself had stamped 'Legal and Confidential' two years earlier. Within it, there were 216 letters Nobel had written to a Miss Sofie Hess. There were also forty letters from Sofie to Nobel, a single well-written telegram, a photogravure of the couple, as well as one affidavit assuring the Nobel estate that Sofie 'had no further claims against the estate apart from the annual income designated to her.' Of note, some of Nobel's letters to Sofie were addressed to 'Dear, pretty child,' 'Little Sweetheart,' 'My dearest Sofiechen' and even 'Frau Sofie Nobel.'

The awkward details were as follows: In 1876, a forty-three-year-old Nobel had met the much younger Sofie – then representing herself as eighteen years old[15] – at a spa in a small Austrian resort. Sofie was working in a florist shop but aspired to advance beyond her lower-middle-class Viennese background. Nobel, enthralled by Sofie's beauty, offered assistance. Assuming a role akin to an avuncular patron, Nobel installed his protégée in a small but comfortable Paris apartment. Sofie was then provided with a substantial allowance intended to further her education. Although Sofie neglected her studies, Nobel fell in love. The infatuation would last fifteen years, fluctuating substantially in its intensity and warmth. At times, Nobel was jealous;[16] at other times he was more concerned that Sofie was wasting her life with an 'old philosopher' like himself. Nobel's largesse could also waver. Most often indulgent, he was also capable of railing against Sofie's extravagant and heavily subsidized lifestyle.

15. She was, in fact, twenty-five.

16. 'Jealous' is an understatement. Nobel frequently accused Sofie of consorting with other men and at times his accusations reached delusional proportions. After receiving a cable from Sofie that was unusually well-written, Nobel became particularly incensed: 'It doesn't require much wit to guess who put together the telegram you sent me. He doesn't write badly, but even so there are mistakes.' The suspected suitor was a Professor Gösta Mittag-Leffler, a leading Swedish mathematician. Historians continue to argue whether Nobel's failure to designate a prize for mathematics in his will was due to the animosity he felt for Mittag-Leffler.

Figure 9. Sofie Hess.

Though Nobel would insist to others that his association with Sofie was platonic, the two often travelled together and, with Nobel's collusion, Sofie would at times represent herself as Madame Nobel. Ultimately, their relationship cooled and by the late 1880s Sofie had returned to Austria and begun openly to entertain other men. In July 1891, she had a daughter out of wedlock. She eventually married the Hungarian father, a Captain von Kapivar, in 1895. By then, Nobel had established a fixed annuity of six thousand Hungarian florins for Sofie, albeit with the following admonition:

> *It is clear to everyone who knows the circumstances that you have been extremely lucky. Most men in my position would have calmly left you to the misery you have brought upon yourself.*

Despite the generous support, both Sofie and Captain von Kapivar began to beg Nobel for an increase in her allowance. With the assistance of a lawyer, Sofie's petitions continued after Nobel's death. These were now directed to Nobel's executors (i.e., Sohlman) and with a more threatening tone: if increased funds were not forthcoming, Nobel's highly personal letters to Sofie would be sold for publication to the highest bidder. Sohlman, anxious to avoid a scandal, negotiated a one-time settlement in return for the affidavit referenced above as well as all outstanding letters from Nobel in Sofie's possession.

The distasteful nature of Sofie's demands left Sohlman puzzled as to how a man as sophisticated as Nobel could have fallen in love with such an ill-suited woman. One explanation for Nobel's puzzling infatuation with Sofie relates to his fragile psychological state at the time of their initial meeting. A few months prior to encountering Sofie, Nobel had taken out the Victorian equivalent of a classified advertisement in a Viennese newspaper: 'A wealthy and highly educated old gentleman living in Paris seeks to engage a mature lady with language proficiency as secretary and housekeeper.' The successful applicant was a thirty-three-year-old Austrian woman, Countess Bertha Kinsky von Chinic und Tettau. The aristocratic title was misleading. Bertha was a poor cousin within an otherwise prominent family and was then working as a governess in the home of the wealthy Baron Karl von Suttner. After travelling by train to Paris, Bertha was met by Nobel, who then escorted his new employee to comfortable quarters in a nearby hotel. Nobel appears to have fallen instantly in love. By all accounts, Bertha was beautiful and sophisticated. She was fluent in four languages. She shared Nobel's love of literature and opera.[17] She, in turn, appears to have been pleasantly surprised by her new circumstances: 'Alfred Nobel made a very good impression on me. He was certainly anything but the "old gentleman" described in the advertisement.'

Unknown to Nobel, Bertha arrived in Paris still deeply attached to Arthur Gundaccar von Suttner, the son of her recent employer and seven years younger than herself. After only one week of employment, Bertha returned to Vienna so that she and Arthur could elope. Nobel was heartbroken. Despite their limited acquaintance, he had already indulged in fantasies about their life together, including the renovations that would be required to accommodate a married couple within his elegant Parisian mansion on Avenue

---

17. Nobel's only disappointment was Bertha's unfamiliarity with a Remington typewriter.

Figure 10. Bertha von Suttner.

Malakoff. Reeling from the pain of unrequited love,[18] Nobel retreated to a spa in Austria. It was there that he met Sofie and her easily won affection.

Sohlman, not completely naive, eventually concluded that Sofie represented more than a timely remedy for Nobel's injured self-esteem. There was also the matter of Nobel's more 'basic' needs. In Sohlman's words, Sofie was adeptly prepared to do 'everything possible to amuse and entertain him.'

Years later, Nobel would again find himself in the lingering lonely aftermath of a failed relationship, this time with Sofie as the rejecting figure. Once again, Nobel would turn to a younger woman for affection.

---

18. Freud, never one to look at life through rose coloured glasses, viewed all love as unrequited.

CHAPTER 5

STONEHENGE FOR SALE

Among Nobel's personal papers was a series of letters involving a correspondent by the name of Florence Antrobus. It was a forename *and* surname that Sohlman immediately recognized. In late January 1894, Sohlman had accompanied Nobel on a brief trip to London. Nobel had been scheduled to appear before the House of Lords, then England's highest court, as a plaintiff in the so-called Cordite Case. The proceedings were the legal culmination of a bitter dispute that arose from Nobel's invention of a smokeless explosive powder that he had patented in 1877 as ballistite. In 1899, two British scientists (who had been former associates of Nobel) proceeded with their own patent for a compound, which they named cordite. As cordite was virtually identical to ballistite, Nobel was suing for patent infringement.

After completing two days of testimony in London, Nobel asked Sohlman to join him on a short excursion. Until then, Sohlman had been unaware that Nobel was actively looking to procure a substantial tract of land in England in order to test cannons, missiles and other large-scale armaments. With some excitement, Nobel had read

19. Nobel lost the lengthy legal proceedings, an unexpected outcome and one that further fuelled his bitter disillusionment with the legal system.

of an interesting opportunity on the Salisbury Plain in Wiltshire, about eighty-five miles from London. It was the headline in London's *Evening News* that had captured Nobel's attention: 'Stonehenge for sale!' Although the majestic stone ruins were highlighted in the accompanying advertisement, Nobel had also noticed that 1,300 acres of adjoining land would be associated with the purchase. As Nobel had yet to establish a foothold in the English explosives industry, he was intent on inspecting the acreage for sale as soon as possible.

Nobel and Sohlman visited the property in early February 1894. Acting as principal host and guide was Sir Edmund Antrobus, Third Baronet of Antrobus and proprietor of the estate.[20] The baronet was a 'motivated' seller. Although proud to preside over what those in the Antrobus family referred to as the 'great relic,' the associated responsibilities had become tedious. Of primary concern was the onslaught of visitors, many of whom were intent on removing stones as souvenirs or desecrating those still remaining. There were other frustrations. Unstable stones had to be propped up with scaffolding; horse manure was everywhere; the burrows of rabbits and rodents were literally undermining the monument's safety; and the baronet increasingly resented the incessant and often patronizing requests from those who wished to explore and excavate the site, all of which he refused.

The additional sad reality was that the baronet needed money. Despite the illusion of wealth, he was badly in debt due to a combination of poor investments and the need to maintain 'appearances,' which for the baronet meant a large

---

20. Baronet is a hereditary title of the lowest order but entitling the bearer and his wife to be addressed as Sir and Lady, respectively.

servant staff and a far-too-lavish home. The latter was Amesbury Abbey, located some two miles from Stonehenge in the village of Amesbury. The baronet had spent his inheritance building the three-storey mansion with its imposing loggia on the site of the original abbey that had been destroyed by fire. At the time of Nobel's visit, the sizeable residence was then home to nine servants in addition to the baronet, his wife and an assortment of near and distant relations.

Once pleasantries had been exchanged with the baronet, the inspection proceeded. Despite the frailty of his sixty years and the chilly February weather, Nobel successfully utilized various vantage points and a commandeered horse-driven carriage to survey a great deal of the property. Nobel's opinion was favourable: though he shielded his impressions from the baronet, he immediately recognized that the countryside surrounding Stonehenge would serve as an ideal artillery range. The appraisal ended at the 'great relic' itself. There, the baronet had prearranged the presence and assistance of his daughter-in-law Florence, who was among those family members who lived at Amesbury Abbey.

Florence was an unusually gifted and intelligent woman. Her wealthy father had died by suicide when she was seven, leaving her mother, Georgina, to raise her and two younger sisters. Thanks to Georgina's progressive attitude and an extensive trust fund that afforded the best tutors, Florence's education included not only the 'domestic' pursuits and English poetry and prose, a typical curriculum for a woman of her time, but also subjects such as mathematics and science, which were then largely reserved for males. Much to Georgina's pleasure, Florence excelled at her studies and was to be one of the first female graduates of Bedford

College at the University of London. It was there that Florence met the baronet's eldest son (also named Edmund) and, after a courtship unusually extended due to Edmund's military service in the Sudan, the couple married in 1886. Florence had then set aside her aspirations to teach English literature and settled, a little uncomfortably, into a traditional Victorian marriage.

At the time of Nobel's visit, Florence's husband was still active in the Grenadier Guards and was stationed in London as Brevet Colonel of the Third Battalion. The couple's only child, then seven, was also in London as a boarding student at a boys' preparatory school.[21] Despite such separations from her husband and son, Florence was content living in Amesbury. She had developed a profound connection to the countryside and often walked to Stonehenge to admire the old stones. There, she would spend hours sketching, in her words, their 'dark, mysterious forms' at different hours of the day or, in a series of notebooks, writing the poems that the 'magic of Stonehenge' had inspired.

At the baronet's request, Florence carefully escorted Nobel and Sohlman between the upright and fallen stones, sharing her knowledge of Stonehenge as they proceeded. She particularly wanted Nobel and Sohlman to appreciate the beauty of their surroundings, and described in great detail how the stones changed their colours with the shifting weather. Florence also provided a charming overview of the various theories addressing how Stonehenge had arisen. The earliest of these was a medieval legend that implicated the conjurations of Merlin the Magician.

---

21. In keeping with Antrobus family tradition, Florence's son was also named Edmund.

Subsequent 'experts' ascribed Stonehenge to the work of invading armies, most often the Romans or the Danes. According to Florence, the most popular current belief was that the Druids, the most prominent priests of ancient Britain, had erected Stonehenge as a temple. Pointing dramatically to a large flat stone lying on the ground, Florence ended the walkabout by announcing in a hushed voice, 'it was upon this very Slaughter Stone that the Druids practised their ritual of human sacrifice.' Taking Nobel by the hand to steady his stride, Florence then cheerily provided her own *caveat emptor*: she herself was uncertain if any of the explanations were true and preferred simply to delight in the splendour and mystery of Stonehenge.

Nobel was captivated by Florence's performance (or, as Sohlman would later assert, by Florence herself). After posing a number of questions related to whether the missing stones might have been deliberately demolished and, if so, how, Nobel then insisted on briskly climbing the wooden scaffolding supporting the tallest of the upright stones. The elevation afforded Nobel a splendid view of the adjoining acreage as well as the nearby River Avon.[22]

As Nobel thanked Florence, he surprised her by quoting from Lord Byron's epic poem *Don Juan*, 'The Druids' groves are gone – so much the better.' Just as unexpectedly, Florence quickly finished the couplet, 'Stone-Henge is not – but what the devil is it?' To their delight, the two quickly discovered that both loved the English Romantic poets, Byron best of all. Sohlman was astonished. He had no idea that Nobel had read and memorized a great deal of poetry during his adolescence in St. Petersburg. Moreover, when

---

22. The bravado also brought on severe chest pain.

Florence shyly confided that she was also attempting to convey 'feebly in words' her poetic impressions of Stonehenge, Nobel shared that he, too, had once written poetry as a young man. Unlike his own failed literary aspirations, however, Nobel assured Florence that he was certain it would one day be his pleasure to read her verse in print.

On returning to the continent, Nobel offered to purchase Stonehenge and the advertised acreage. Serious negotiations continued by both letter and telegram over the next few weeks. In dispute was the issue of grazing rights, which the baronet had hoped to maintain. Nobel was amused. Unless the baronet secretly intended to establish an outdoor abattoir, the presence of browsing sheep was dangerously incompatible with Nobel's own intention of using the property as an oversized firing range. Though the baronet would concede this point, there was still the contentious matter of the purchase price. The baronet was demanding £125,000. Given that downland was then worth only £10 per acre, it meant the ancient monument itself was being valued at over £100,000, a price Nobel viewed as highly inflated. Nevertheless, as Nobel had found himself strangely attracted to the presence of the old stones,[23] his counter-offer was a still generous £90,000. The difference would soon become a moot point.

Within days of his visit, rumours had reached Westminster that Nobel was about to acquire Stonehenge. Unfortunately for Nobel, there was now mounting concern throughout the United Kingdom that wealthy foreigners

---

23. It was Freud who originated the term 'displacement,' a defence mechanism in which one object is substituted for another, such as when a person shifts his/her sexual impulses from an unacceptable or unobtainable target to one more acceptable or obtainable, either animate or inanimate in nature.

Figure 11. Stonehenge.

were seeking to buy structures of national importance just to dismantle them, either for the worth of their components or in order to transport and re-erect them upon foreign soil. The precipitant for such apprehension was the recent sale of Tattershall Castle in Lincolnshire. A consortium of American entrepreneurs had purchased the castle, only to remove its twenty-eight medieval stone fireplaces for immediate sale across the Atlantic. Members of Parliament and peers of the House of Lords, previously more concerned with the property rights of private citizens, were finally recognizing the importance of preserving England's historic monuments and properties. With the sale of Stonehenge to Nobel apparently on the horizon, and with no certainty of Nobel's intentions, the British politicians acted quickly.

In early March 1894, the Parliament of the United Kingdom introduced the *Ancient Monuments Protection Act*. Although the Act was designed principally to preclude the injury or defacement of historic buildings and monuments, there was an additional caveat: the owner of any 'ancient monument' scheduled in the Act was no longer permitted to sell or gift the monument of interest to anyone other than a citizen or agency of the United Kingdom. Prominent on the list of sixty-eight prehistoric monuments mentioned specifically in the Act was 'the group of stones known as Stonehenge, Amesbury, Wiltshire.'

Nobel was indignant. Though he had assured the baronet he had no intention of razing Stonehenge, he was well aware of the Act's ramifications. Despite both men's disappointment, there was little choice but to amicably end the negotiations.

Florence's first letter to Nobel was dated two months later.

CHAPTER 6

FLORENCE ANTROBUS

Amesbury Abbey
3 May 1894

Dear Mr. Nobel,

I do hope you remember our meeting. I had the recent pleasure of introducing you to the grandeur of Stonehenge, those magnificent stones just beyond our Amesbury home. I confess I was pleased to hear that you are no longer their suitor, but not because you would be their unworthy guardian. No – it is only because I would miss the old stones so desperately, though they no longer stand as proud as they once did in ancient days.

I trust you do not think it overfamiliar of me to mention that I still recall with delight our spirited discussion – not only of Stonehenge but of Shelley and Wordsworth and, of course, our dear Lord Byron.

Mr. Nobel: when you departed, you encouraged my literary pursuits, fanciful as they may be, and I turn to you now for advice. Would you see fit to share your thoughts on the enclosed verse and prose? If so, you will find I have attempted to express my profound sentiments for the poetical aspects of Stonehenge. I hope I am not overstepping propriety by making this request, but I sensed in you a shared love of the written word – and I hope of Stonehenge itself.

Regardless of your interest in my minor ambitions, I do trust I can write to you from time to time. I am concerned about your health and encourage you to dress more warmly when outside.

Sincerely,
Florence C. M. Antrobus

P.S. Since your visit, the baronet has received no other offers for Stonehenge. Indeed, the Inspector of Ancient Monuments[24] has recently arrived – unannounced! – and has now presented the baronet with a 'Preservation Order.' A number of stones must immediately be made safe, at the baronet's expense, and the roadway for wheeled traffic that runs through the monument must be diverted. It is apparently now our legal 'duty' to preserve Stonehenge. The baronet is furious; he is convinced the ongoing costs of upkeep will now jeopardize any chance of selling Stonehenge. I am, on the other hand, enormously happy!

Nobel was relieved. The vast majority of the correspondence he received was what he would refer to as 'begging letters' – i.e., from individuals in difficult personal circumstances, funding campaigns to raise statues, and so on. It was therefore with genuine pleasure and interest that Nobel read Florence's letter and the enclosures it contained: a small packet of poems, six in all, and a short piece of pastoral prose detailing the sun's passage through the stones.

Nobel's letter of response, written in English, arrived in mid-July, just over two months later.

---

24. General Augustus Henry Lane-Fox Pitt-Rivers, the first Inspector of Ancient Monuments under the 1894 *Ancient Monuments Protection Act*.

Dear Miss[25] *Antrobus,*

I most certainly remember our meeting at Stonehenge. Your charming tour made a great impression upon me and my thoughts have returned on more than one occasion to the delightful time we spent together. I was fortunate indeed to have such a well-informed guide.

And now to receive your wonderful poetry and prose. Thank you for entrusting me with it. I am far from a worthy critic, but I read all you enclosed with interest and admiration. I must again encourage you to publish your work one day. Your talents must not be wasted only on me!

And now a request of you. Though I first regretted my failure to acquire Stonehenge, I am now relieved I have not deprived you of your muse. However I believe the Inspector is correct; it was also my impression that the taller stones are in imminent danger of falling. Would you and your family do me the honour of accepting a contribution toward the costs incurred by the 'Preservation Order'? As I wish to see the stones again one day – and their gracious docent – it is in MY selfish interest that this offer be accepted.

My warmest greetings to your husband and the Baronet. I remain,

A. Nobel

Florence replied immediately, thanking Nobel for his generous words. She hoped, of course, that Nobel would

---

25. 'Freudian slip': an unintentional error revealing an unconscious wish.

indeed visit again, perhaps in the fall, when he might experience 'the wild, tempestuous autumnal gales that usually sweep across the Plain in October.' She was firm, however, on declining any financial support for Stonehenge. As she conveyed to Nobel, the baronet, a proud man, would simply hear of no such assistance.

Although they would not, in fact, meet again, Florence continued to write to Nobel at regular intervals. In between descriptions of life at Amesbury Abbey, there began to appear more personal asides, including a diffident sharing of her husband's prolonged absences and the growing burden of her loneliness. Most often, however, Florence wrote about Stonehenge. Emboldened by Nobel's praise, she soon divulged that she had decided to write a 'sentimental' guide to Stonehenge, one that she hoped a traveller to Stonehenge might find 'pleasure in reading.' It would contain her 'poetical and picturesque' impressions of Stonehenge, such as found in the following letter:

Amesbury Abbey
3 April 1895

Dear Mr. Alfred Nobel,

Late this morning I walked to Stonehenge. Though I have visited the exquisitely coloured stones a thousand times before, I have never failed to be moved by their startling, sudden presence. For even from the banks of the nearby River Avon, the old stones are at first nowhere to be seen. Yet as one moves determinedly through the crackling grass and up the winding valley with the turquoise spring flowers signalling the traveller's way, the tallest of the stones suddenly appear! Those nearest

join together in a large outer circle – as if each was hold-
ing another's hands – and together the ancient stones
stand in defiant solidarity against the onslaught of time.

I stayed until evening. The sense of peace and tran-
quility are with me still.

Ever sincerely,
Florence Antrobus

Though not as prolific a correspondent as Florence, Nobel's responses were always courteous and gracious. He was genuinely admiring of Florence's 'poetical' powers of observation. But Nobel's intrinsic inquisitiveness and pragmatism also led to more prosaic questions.

Björkborn Manor
13 July 1895

Dear Florence, (I trust I may name you so?)

Thank you for your recent letters. It is particularly exciting to hear news of your intention to publish a 'senti-mental' guide to Stonehenge. I can think of no better wordsmith to capture the varying moods and colours of the 'great relic.' But might your 'sentimental' guide also be a 'practical' one – a compilation of the facts and consid-erations of learned authorities on the subject of Stone-henge? From where did the stones arise? What purpose lay behind this ancient structure? Who were the people who built these circles? I still recall with pleasure your entertaining account of such matters during my visit to Stonehenge. Might you now explore these questions in a more methodical and scholarly way? It is my view that true knowledge emerges only by careful and detached study, preferably by examining the words and works of those who are cleverer than one self.

But no more preaching! I have news that may interest you. I am now settled at Björkborn Manor and have shared your interest in Stonehenge with the local antiquarians. It appears there is a place in southern Sweden where many larger boulders also stand – but in the shape of an ancient ship. It is known as the Ales Stenar.

Perhaps one day I will have the pleasure of providing you with a tour of our *country's Stonehenge?*

Sincerely,
A. N.

P.S. Please accept my gift of a Remington typewriter. It is a selfish gesture on my part as I take such delight in reading your tidings of Stonehenge.

Florence was pleased to learn of *Ales Stenar*. She was even more delighted to receive the typewriter. Taking Nobel's suggestions seriously, she began to gather and read all existing accounts that touched upon Stonehenge, forwarding to Nobel facts of particular interest. In response, Nobel's next gift was a camera.[26] He was now encouraging Florence to document the general appearance of

---

26. In 1895, Nobel was in the midst of perfecting an airborne camera that could be attached to a miniature parachute and shot into the air by rocket. While aloft, the camera's shutter could be opened with a small time-delayed fuse-detonated explosion that would trigger both a film exposure and the parachute's deployment. The descending camera would then be tracked and its aerial photograph retrieved. Although most of the cameras failed to survive their ordeal, Nobel (correctly) believed that such photographs might one day be successfully used to monitor enemy manoeuvres (as occurred during the photo-reconnaissance flights of World War I).

Figure 12. Florence Antrobus.

Stonehenge, not only by providing descriptions of the individual stones, but by including relevant illustrations and photographs. In thanking Nobel, Florence included not only photographs of Stonehenge but also a keepsake of her own likeness.

Nobel was, of course, deeply touched by Florence's personal photo and her appreciation. However, it would be some time before he would write again. After the summer at Björkborn Manor, Nobel had travelled south to Paris. That fall, he began to experience bouts of severe chest pain. Nobel was hospitalized against his protestations and then spent two months confined to his Paris mansion. It was a contemplative Nobel who wrote Florence from Paris in November 1895.

5 November 1895
Paris

Dear Florence,

I'm afraid my delay in writing is by Doctor's orders. My heart troubles are severe and I have been ordered to bed. The spirits of Niflheim *have descended and one of my few pleasures has been to receive your letters and the accompanying photographs. Indeed, it has given me great satisfaction to see you are progressing with your account of Stonehenge. Your book will be a lasting and noteworthy legacy, one that travellers to Stonehenge will find useful and inspiring in the years ahead.*

Lately I, too, have been considering my contribution to posterity. As I am certain I am much more unwell than my doctors suspect, I wish to ensure I have made my bequests to those who are dear to me. I am now in

*the process of rewriting my Last Will and Testament.
May I include you in some way? Your letters have meant
a great deal to me, and I have valued our growing
friendship, a rare treasure in my life of loneliness. You
have been steadfast in refusing any monies for you or
your family. But is there something that you might accept
from a friend?*

*Sincerely,
Alfred*

*P.S. I am staring at your lovely face as I write this letter.
This photograph is one of the dearest gifts I have ever
received.*

Florence initially refused to respond directly to Nobel's
heartfelt enquiry, assuring her friend he had years to live
and that there was no rush in determining bequests of any
kind. Instead, for the next six months, her letters to Nobel
continued in the vein that had been previously established:
impressions of Stonehenge that were now augmented by
an increasing number of photographs and illustrations.

Florence was, in fact, deeply distressed by Nobel's declining health. Due to a temporary improvement in his heart
condition, Nobel was again well enough to summer at
Björkborn Manor in July and August of 1896. That fall,
however, Nobel's angina worsened, and this time he was
more convinced than ever that he was dying. Nobel again
wrote to Florence, insisting she specify what bequest she
was willing to receive from a man near death.

Florence finally responded as follows:

Amesbury Abbey
17 October 1896

Dear Alfred,

I, too, have valued our correspondence and friendship but I am afraid I cannot accept a financial bequest of any kind. As you are insistent, I now have one suggestion. You have honoured me with your interest in my passion – Stonehenge. You have challenged me to go beyond the beauty of Stonehenge and to learn more about its mysterious presence. I have strived vainly to do so – yet I have found so little is known with certitude.

Alfred, you are wise in so many ways – let solving the mystery of Stonehenge be your bequest to me. And, by offering me this gift, let Stonehenge continue to bind us together.

With friendship,
Florence

Florence's letter arrived at a time when Nobel's health had markedly deteriorated. Despite his pain and debilitated state, Nobel immediately replied as follows:

5 November 1896
Paris

Dear Friend,

Your letter of the 17th has now found me in Paris. I have thought seriously of how to respond to your unusual request. I can think of only one solution.

I share in confidence that a year ago I chose to will the bulk of my fortune to the formation of a series of prizes. These will be for worthy individuals whose works have benefited mankind — men and women who have made important scientific discoveries, produced outstanding literary works, championed peace.

In the hope it addresses your request of me, I now plan to will part of my fortune for the creation of an additional prize — to be awarded to the outstanding man or woman amongst these prizewinners who can solve the mystery of Stonehenge.

Sadly, I have concluded it will take a greater and healthier mind than mine to solve the 'great relic.' But there is another reason that draws me to this plan. Until we met, I had always turned to the sciences to further my comprehension of the world and its possibilities. You have taught me that an emotional and 'sentimental' response to what we wish to understand can be just as powerful.

As Stonehenge is both 'Science' and 'Art,' let us therefore draw upon both scientists and artists to solve the mystery of Stonehenge.

With affection,
Alfred

It was the last letter Nobel was to write to Florence. Within a few days Nobel had returned to San Remo where he spent his few remaining weeks attending to several neglected business matters as his health allowed. He was to receive one final letter from Amesbury Abbey:

Amesbury Abbey
25 November 1896

Dear Friend,
You have conceived of a considerable gift for me and a place I hold dearer than anywhere in the world. Yes, you must do this!

With great affection,
Florence

Despite searching carefully, Sohlman could find no further letters between the two, or whether Nobel had in any way acted on his intention to create the prize he had promised Florence. Sohlman did, however, find one further reference to Stonehenge. Nobel's last journal entry, written three days before his death, read as follows:

7 December 1896: I have had the most disturbing – and wonderful – dream. Mid-winter, evening, a time long ago. Together we crossed the river Avon. As we strode unhurriedly toward Stonehenge, ancient songs and chants drifted quietly around us. You steadied me gently as we approached our inevitable destination; your hand under my elbow, your flowing red hair just visible in the fading light. The stones appeared suddenly – like black columns. Tenderly, you laid me down. I was not afraid. I was at peace. The descending darkness of the night was now upon us. The world of the living seemed to be drifting away.[27]

---

27. Freud found the proximity of love and death in a single dream to be a profoundly moving experience – for both the dreamer and the analyst.

CHAPTER 7

THE SECRET CODICIL

S ohlman, shaken by the revelations of these letters and uncertain how to proceed, telegraphed Lilljeqvist and informed his co-executor that a significant new complication had emerged with respect to Nobel's estate.

STOCKHOLM SWEDEN 26 FEB 1901
A SERIES OF LETTERS HAS BEEN FOUND
THAT APPEARS TO ALTER NOBEL'S WILL.
THE MATTER IS A DELICATE AFFAIR.
SOHLMAN

Lilljeqvist's response was immediate. In his return telegram, he suggested that Sohlman forward copies of the correspondence in question to Lindhagen for his legal opinion. Once Lindhagen had examined the material, Lilljeqvist would be willing to travel from his home in Bengtsfors to Stockholm to help resolve any outstanding difficulties. As usual, Lilljeqvist's advice proved helpful. Lindhagen's memorandum was written ten days later and read as follows:

PRIVATE & CONFIDENTIAL
Privileged

Stockholm
8 March 1901

To the Attention of Ragnar Sohlman and Rudolf Lilljeqvist

RE: Florence Antrobus

As instructed, I have reviewed the Florence Antrobus–Alfred Nobel Correspondence. In total, twenty-two letters – all handwritten in English – were exchanged between Nobel and Florence Antrobus, dating from 3 May 1894 to 25 November 1896. On the assumption the letters are authentic, the matter before us is whether Nobel has written a codicil – that is, a legally enforceable amendment to his existing will.

My considered opinion is as follows:

1. Swedish courts recognize codicils provided they adhere to the same legal standards applicable to a valid will; such standards require the signatures of at least two disinterested witnesses. As Nobel's written intention to will an additional prize for solving the mystery of Stonehenge (the 'Stonehenge' letter, dated 5 November 1896) was not witnessed and was embedded in an otherwise informal and personal letter, it is highly unlikely that any probate court would uphold its validity.

2. The 'Stonehenge' letter was written and signed in Paris, as was Nobel's final iteration of his Last Will and Testament. You will recall it required significant manoeuvring to convince various courts that Nobel's will should be administered in Sweden and not in France. Initiating new court proceedings to clarify the legal implications of a letter signed in France would require revisiting the issue of jurisdiction, conceivably jeopardizing – unwisely in my view – the existing Swedish authority over Nobel's will.

3. There is an additional consideration. Although Nobel has not specified the nature of the prize for 'solving' Stonehenge, it would follow that any monetary award ascribed to the winning 'solution' would diminish the worth of the residuum of Nobel's estate. By extension, the available funds for the residuary beneficiaries would also decrease and such interested parties – i.e., members of Nobel's family and the various prize-awarding bodies – would no doubt seek to challenge the validity of any putative codicil put before the courts.

It would be prudent to discuss the matter further. May I suggest my office, 25 March at 4 p.m.

Sincere via[28]
Carl Lindhagen

The three men met as Lindhagen had proposed. After Sohlman recounted how both he and Nobel had first met Florence Antrobus, Lindhagen reviewed the key points of his memorandum. In Lilljeqvist's view, the resolution of the matter was now straightforward: the Florence Antrobus–Nobel correspondence should be ignored or, better yet, destroyed at once.

Sohlman, however, was hesitant. Although he valued Lindhagen's legal counsel, Sohlman's intimate familiarity with *all* of Nobel's correspondence had aroused a strong sense of déjà vu.[29] Unlike his two colleagues, Sohlman was

---

28. Esperanto translation: Best wishes.

29. For Freud, déjà vu – the sense that an event or perception currently being experienced has already taken place – represented the unexpected reminder of a repressed desire. The most severe case of déjà vu that Freud encountered was when a newly referred patient abruptly discontinued treatment. When Freud sought an explanation, he learned that the patient was convinced he had already

Figure 13. Carl Lindhagen.

well aware that Bertha von Suttner and Nobel also began an amiable exchange of letters after she had left Nobel's employment in 1876. Once Bertha became more involved in the anti-war movement, she shared this interest with Nobel and also petitioned his financial support for various initiatives related to promoting peace. Soon, Nobel was financially contributing to her efforts as well as offering his own views on whether the international peace movement would succeed. Nobel eventually determined to leave a part of his estate toward a prize for peace. As he wrote to Bertha in 1893,

> *I should like to will part of my fortune to the creation of prizes to be distributed every five years (let us say six times in a row, for if in thirty years, humanity has not succeeded in reforming society as it is now, we shall surely fall once again into barbarism) to the man or woman who has most effectively contributed to bringing peace to Europe.*

Although the terms for this prize would change considerably, Nobel honoured his commitment to peace in his final will. In view of these analogous events, Sohlman was quite convinced that Nobel had also intended to honour his commitment to Stonehenge but had simply been too busy or too ill (and more likely the latter) to alter his final will. The implications of that conclusion, at least for Sohlman, were clear: all three men now had, if not a legal obligation, then surely an ethical obligation to act on Nobel's intentions to solve the mystery of Stonehenge.

undergone years of psychoanalysis with Freud, and was prepared to produce receipts to that effect. In what almost amounted to a folie à déjà vu deux, Freud initially wondered if he had indeed treated the patient. In the end, Freud simply regretted the loss of income.

Although Lindhagen now saw the merit of Sohlman's argument, Lilljeqvist was still sceptical. He could understand why Nobel had chosen to establish prizes for chemistry, physics and physiology or medicine. As Lilljeqvist had known Nobel as a cultured and well-read man, he was also not surprised that Nobel had designated a prize for literature. Lilljeqvist could even view the prize for peace as a logical extension of Nobel's interests, particularly on learning of Nobel's acquaintance with Bertha von Suttner. But he was now being asked to contemplate an idiosyncratic and circumscribed prize for solving the mystery of how stone circles came to stand in a foreign land. For Lilljeqvist, a bequest involving Stonehenge seemed too far removed from Nobel's otherwise-known testamentary intentions of rewarding those who had already made significant contributions in the sciences, humanities and society for the benefit of all mankind.

It was then that Sohlman realized it would be helpful to emphasize one additional observation. When Nobel first met Bertha von Suttner she was young and beautiful. When Nobel first met Sofie Hess she was also young and beautiful. And as Sohlman knew first hand, when Nobel first met Florence Antrobus she, too, was young and beautiful. It was clear to Sohlman that a lonely Nobel had again fallen in love. It was just as clear that Nobel's interest in Stonehenge was his way, perhaps his only way, of expressing his love for Florence. As Sohlman eloquently argued, it was a love that must be honoured.[30]

---

30. Sohlman had intuitively grasped what Freud would later expand upon in his 1914 article on 'Repetition compulsion': the unconscious repetition of behaviour patterns throughout life (Freud, 'Remembering, Repeating and Working-Through,' 1914).

As Lilljeqvist stared at the photograph of Florence that Sohlman had just presented to him, he, too, now recognized the truth of Sohlman's appraisal: there was no arguing with love. The new challenge was to remain true to the moral imperative of respecting Nobel's wishes without undermining the fragile legal underpinnings of Nobel's entire legacy. After further discussion, the three men decided upon the following course of action. First and foremost, Nobel's plan to solve the mystery of Stonehenge would be respected. However, the decision to award what they would now refer to as the Stonehenge Prize would be considered a strictly private matter. That is, the Stonehenge Prize would not be deemed equivalent to one of the five prizes established in Nobel's will, nor would the Stonehenge Prize be associated in any way with the Nobel Foundation or the existing Nobel prize-awarding bodies. Instead, it was to be a prize *in memory of* Alfred Nobel that the three men would establish as their own collective and private tribute to a man they wished to honour.

As Sohlman had been the strongest advocate for acting on Nobel's intentions, he volunteered to oversee the adjudication of the prize on behalf of all three men. Lilljeqvist quickly accepted the offer. After four years of participating in time-consuming and challenging negotiations, he had little time or inclination to engage in further duties involving Nobel's legacy. Lindhagen was also in agreement, particularly as he now saw the men's responsibility as ethical, not legal. There was the matter, however, of an appropriate monetary prize, especially as it was now established that the initial valuation of each of the five Nobel Prizes (as they were now known) would be over 150,000 Swedish kronor. Lilljeqvist proposed that half the remuneration he had received as an executor of Nobel's estate (i.e., 25,000 Swedish kronor) be put toward the Stonehenge Prize. Lindhagen was equally generous. He had been well compensated as the executors' legal counsel and would also contribute 25,000 Swedish kronor. So too, in the end, would Sohlman.[31] With a total of 75,000 Swedish kronor now available, 15,000 Swedish kronor would be set aside to underwrite expenses associated with the adjudication process while the prize itself would be worth a respectable 60,000 Swedish kronor.

The meeting ended with the three men making a sombre toast to the memory of Alfred Nobel, followed by the customary four cheers. Sohlman then proposed a second toast. Four years earlier, at a time when the likelihood of successfully executing Nobel's will had seemed remote, Emanuel Nobel had encouraged Sohlman with the following words:

Always keep in mind the meaning of the Russian word for an executor – 'Dusie Prikaztjik, *the vicar of the soul' – and try to act accordingly.*

'*Dusie Prikaztjik*' had since become the men's private rallying cry. Led by Sohlman, the three men – now raucously – chanted in unison: '*Dusie Prikaztjik! Dusie Prikaztjik! Dusie Prikaztjik!*'

It was Lilljeqvist's voice that rang out loudest.

---

31. As Sohlman's compensation as executor was twice that of Lilljeqvist's, he had initially thought it more equitable to contribute a greater sum. He was finally convinced otherwise, but only because Lilljeqvist and Lindhagen were insistent that the significant amount of time that Sohlman would now devote to the matter on their behalf must also be recognized as a substantial contribution.

CHAPTER 8

THE ROYAL SWEDISH ACADEMY OF LETTERS, HISTORY AND ANTIQUITIES

Sohlman's first task was to establish an adjudication process. As he had just spent over four years successfully negotiating with the Swedish Academy, the Royal Swedish Academy of Sciences, the Karolinska Institute and the Norwegian Parliament, Sohlman was reasonably confident of a satisfactory outcome. Despite initial strong reservations and differences about how the prizes designated in Nobel's will were to be awarded, all parties had agreed to a hard-fought, but amicable, solution. In brief, there were to be Nobel Committees appointed by each of the four institutions; these would be responsible for eliciting and reviewing the official nominations. Generally, the responsibility of the small committees would be to provide a reasoned opinion to the broader membership of their respective institutions, who would then vote to determine the winning recipient. In the case of the Nobel Peace Prize, however, the Norwegian Nobel Committee would independently determine the prizewinner. Sohlman reasonably foresaw that this same evaluation and decision-making structure could apply, *mutatis mutandis*, to the manner in which the Stonehenge Prize was awarded.

After reading a number of popular accounts of Stonehenge, Sohlman determined that the principal area of adjudicating expertise for the Stonehenge Prize should lie within the blurred fields of the antiquities and archaeology. Sohlman was also certain that he wanted to engage a Swedish institution to adjudicate the prize. Cognizant of the patriotic outcry aroused by Nobel's decision to turn to the Norwegian Parliament as a prize-awarding body, Sohlman had no appetite to repeat Nobel's circumvention of parochial Swedish interests.

With the above considerations in mind, Sohlman discreetly learned of only two Swedish-based institutions that merited consideration. One was the Royal Swedish Academy of Letters, History and Antiquities (hereafter referred to as the Royal Academy of Letters), a learned society established in 1786 by King Gustav III and derived from an earlier institution founded by Gustav's mother, Queen Lovisa Ulrika. The other was the Swedish Antiquarian Society, a much less formal organization founded in 1869 by those who privately collected Nordic artefacts, then a popular pastime in Sweden. Although the principal aims of both bodies related to historical and antiquarian studies, Sohlman chose to pursue serious discussions with the Royal Academy of Letters as he was swayed by how closely that institution resembled both the Swedish Academy and the Royal Swedish Academy of Sciences in its stature and organizational structure.[32]

Sohlman's initial contact with the Royal Academy of Letters was by way of Oscar Montelius, one of Sweden's

---

32. Sohlman had also learned that most members of the Swedish Antiquarian Society were plundering dilettantes.

most renowned and important archaeologists.[33] The two men had met in the context of their recent appointments to the newly established Board of Directors of the Nobel Foundation. Sohlman was one of three board directors while Montelius had been appointed one of two associates. As Montelius was also a member of the Royal Academy of Letters, Sohlman discreetly canvassed his interest and advice. Montelius was immediately intrigued by the connection to Stonehenge. During his student years at Uppsala University, he had been taught that Stonehenge had been built by invading Danish Vikings in the eighth and ninth centuries, largely based on the supposed similarities between rudimentary stone circles still extant in Denmark and those found at Stonehenge. Although he now viewed any connection between the Vikings and Stonehenge as highly dubious, Montelius had retained an interest in the alleged origins of Stonehenge, and had once journeyed there during an archaeological field trip to the British Isles in 1892.

In his preliminary discussions with Sohlman, Montelius was most troubled by the lack of precision inherent in Nobel's instructions. Accustomed to hearing such reservations, Sohlman assured Montelius that appropriate clarifications to the process of awarding the prize could be fashioned in due course, ideally under Montelius's leadership. To illustrate his point, Sohlman asked Montelius to

33. Montelius is best known for developing a variety of archaeological dating methods. One of his techniques was to organize prehistoric time sequences based on the slowly changing forms of archaeological materials. Thomas Darwin, Charles Darwin's youngest son, was one of many scientists influenced by Montelius's approach. Thomas Darwin went on to propose theories of evolution, analogous to his father's but applicable to inanimate objects, particularly eating utensils (see *The Evolution of Inanimate Objects: The Life and Collected Works of Thomas Darwin [1857–1879]*).

Figure 14. Oscar Montelius.

consider those Stonehenge Prizes that he himself might have previously awarded. A diverted Montelius was quickly able to list the following recipients: Geoffrey of Monmouth, Inigo Jones, John Aubrey and William Stukeley.[34]

Sohlman's ploy worked perfectly, as Montelius was both amused and reassured. Montelius did, however, raise one final concern. New knowledge pertaining to Stonehenge was accruing with each passing year. Was the Stonehenge Prize to be awarded annually? If not, would the more recent winner of a Nobel Prize not be significantly advantaged? It was an issue with which Sohlman, Lilljeqvist and Lindhagen had already struggled. Anxious to respect Nobel's intentions but equally anxious to obtain closure on the competition, they had already determined that the Stonehenge Prize would be awarded only once, with eligibility limited to those individuals who had won Nobel Prizes between the years 1901 and 1910, inclusive. The deadline for all submissions would be 10 December 1911, after which there would be a single adjudication process.

With Sohlman's encouragement, Montelius now approached the constituency of the Royal Academy of Letters for the needed approval to proceed. He was not entirely forthcoming. In order to conceal Nobel's involvement, as Sohlman had insisted, Montelius had agreed to

---

34. Geoffrey of Monmouth recorded the first detailed account of the putative nature and origins of Stonehenge (around 1138 CE); Inigo Jones, an architect and Royal Surveyor of King James I in the 1600s, was the first to measure the monument, albeit inaccurately; John Aubrey, a seventeenth-century antiquarian, discovered what are now known as the 'Aubrey holes' – fifty-six holes dug at regular intervals inside the interior of the bank that surrounds Stonehenge; William Stukeley was the first to consider the importance of Stonehenge's surrounding landscape. Stukeley also published *Stonehenge, A Temple Restored to the British Druids* (1740), popularizing the belief that Stonehenge was a temple of the Druids.

present the Stonehenge Prize as the bequest of an anonymous Swedish citizen. Despite Montelius's advocacy, the majority of academy members were, at first, hesitant. Lack of knowledge, time and resources were each cited as obstacles, as few members of the academy had previously displayed any interest or expertise in matters pertaining to Stonehenge. Others were uneasy with whether the involvement of the Royal Academy of Letters would undermine attention to more parochial concerns: most archaeologists in Sweden were then preoccupied with deciphering Scandinavian variants of the runic alphabet.

Sohlman's reassurances to Montelius aside, there also remained significant doubt as to whether any consensus would emerge with respect to defining the fundamental 'mystery' of Stonehenge. What would be defined as the central question: Was it when, how or why Stonehenge was built? Was it who had built Stonehenge? Was it what Stonehenge represented? Or were there other enigmatic factors to consider? And how was an adjudication committee possibly to determine if a reasonable solution had been provided, regardless of which of the many mysteries was being considered?

In the end, negotiations were concluded successfully, partly due to Montelius's advocacy, but mostly due to monetary considerations. Sohlman had quickly grasped that the Royal Academy of Letters was significantly underfunded and he offered generous terms: each member of the Royal Academy of Letters directly involved in the adjudication process would receive a payment that was then equivalent to a professor's annual salary. In addition, the Royal Academy of Letters as a whole would receive significant funds for its library and chancellery.

It was left to Sohlman and Montelius to work out the details. The two agreed that a three-member committee of the Royal Academy of Letters would carry out the adjudication needed to award the Stonehenge Prize. This committee, to be designated the Stonehenge Prize Committee, would have complete autonomy to decide on what basis to interpret Nobel's intentions and to select the prizewinner. Montelius would chair the committee and select the two additional members. Sohlman would assist the committee by serving as its non-voting secretary. Among his tasks in this capacity, he would inform all eligible Nobel Laureates of their additional opportunity to compete for the Stonehenge Prize. It would also be his responsibility, on behalf of Lilljeqvist, Lindhagen and himself, to present to the winner of the Stonehenge Prize a cheque for 60,000 Swedish kronor. In the interim, 15,000 Swedish kronor would be set aside to fund the work and expertise required for the prize adjudication process; of this amount, 7,500 Swedish kronor would be immediately directed to the Royal Academy of Letters to be used at its discretion.

A slightly embarrassed Montelius raised one last matter. He was aware that members of the Nobel Committees of the prize-awarding institutions identified in Nobel's will were each to receive what was referred to as a Nobel Prize medalet. This was a miniature version of a Nobel Prize medal, though in silver gilt as opposed to twenty-three-carat gold. Montelius requested similar keepsakes for the members of the Stonehenge Prize Committee. As only three medalets would be required, Sohlman graciously agreed.

CHAPTER 9

A SENTIMENTAL AND PRACTICAL GUIDE TO STONEHENGE

On 10 December 1901, Sohlman wrote a confidential and identical letter of invitation to each of the newly anointed Nobel Laureates in physics, chemistry, medicine and physiology, literature and peace. It was a ritual he repeated annually until a last series of letters were issued on 10 December 1910. The letter (translated, as necessary, into the language most appropriate for its recipient) read in English as follows:

Strictly confidential

Dear_____,

I am writing to you as one of the appointed executors of Alfred Nobel's estate. As you are aware, the terms of Alfred Nobel's Last Will and Testament established five prizes of the highest order, to be annually conferred for achievements in the fields of science, literature and the promotion of peace. It has subsequently emerged that it was Alfred Nobel's further wish that those awarded such prizes also be afforded the opportunity to respond to an additional and very specific challenge – hence this present contact. In brief, it was Nobel's intention that an additional prize be established and awarded, 'to the out-

standing man or woman amongst these prizewinners who can solve the mystery of Stonehenge.'

In order to comply with the intentions of Nobel's wish, I have the honour of inviting you to compete for what is now designated the Stonehenge Prize. The additional details pertaining to the competition are as follows:

— Only those prizewinners who forward their solution to the mystery of Stonehenge by way of a brief written submission will be considered for the Stonehenge Prize. This submission, which may be accompanied by documents referred to within, must be received no later than 10 December in the year 1911. No submissions received after that date will be considered.

— An appointed committee of the Royal Swedish Academy of Letters, History and Antiquities will conduct the adjudication.

— The prizewinner will be awarded a cheque in the amount of 60,000 Swedish kronor.

— No further guidance with respect to the Stonehenge Prize will be provided. The envelope containing your submission should be addressed to the undersigned at the address provided below.

As a final comment, please note that any deliberations and opinions related to the prize will not be recorded or divulged. Further, only the prizewinner will be notified of the committee's decision. For a variety of sensitive personal and legal reasons related to Alfred Nobel's legacy, I politely request that this correspondence, and all matters related to the Stonehenge Prize, remain strictly confidential.

Respectfully yours,
Ragnar Sohlman
Norrlandsgatan 6
Stockholm, Sweden

Sohlman's expectations of secrecy may now seem naive. In the earliest years of the Nobel Prizes, however, the names of the new Nobel Laureates were not publicly announced until 10 December, the anniversary of Nobel's death, and the date of the awards ceremony in Stockholm, or in the case of the Peace Prize, in Kristiania, Norway (renamed as Oslo in 1925). This meant that all laureates-to-be, who were privately notified of their prizes usually sometime in late October, were asked not to undermine the dramatic public release of their names at the December ceremony. Almost all winners, grateful for the honour they had received, colluded with this request, even if it meant an unheralded and anonymous arrival in Stockholm or Kristiania in the dead of winter.[35] In view of these prevailing standards for secrecy, Sohlman was confident that the Nobel Laureates would also not hesitate to conceal the existence of the Stonehenge Prize if 'officially' requested.

Indeed, Sohlman was more concerned that many of the Nobel Laureates might have little, if any, prior knowledge of Stonehenge. He, therefore, thought it prudent to include an overview of certain key details of the ancient monument with each laureate's letter of invitation. It was only by chance, however, that Sohlman had acquired the ideal

---

35. There was one outlandish exception. One prizewinner informed seventeen colleagues and ten relatives (some distant), '*in strict confidence – Hurrah! Hurrah!*' – that he would be travelling later that year to Stockholm but that these details were to remain absolutely private until after 10 December.

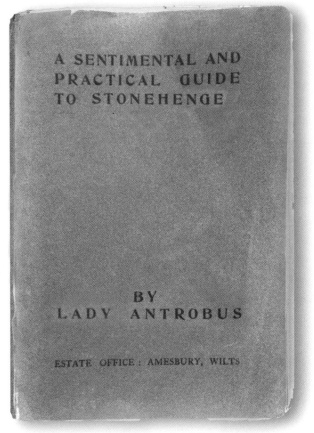

Figure 15. *A Sentimental and Practical Guide to Stonehenge* by Lady Antrobus.

material to circulate. On the legal advice of Lindhagen, Sohlman had written Florence Antrobus once the decision to establish the Stonehenge Prize had been made. (She was by then Lady Florence Antrobus, as her husband had succeeded to the baronetcy on the death of her father-in-law in 1899.) The letter had been deliberately informal in tone. Sohlman had indicated that, as one of the executors of Nobel's will, he had come across correspondence between herself and Mr. Nobel and thereby learned of the mutual interest that she and Mr. Nobel shared in solving the mystery of Stonehenge. Regrettably, as Mr. Nobel had not alluded to this subject in his final will, such interests in the matter of Stonehenge had to be viewed as outside the estate's legal purview. Sohlman, however, wished to inform Lady Antrobus that private efforts would be undertaken to act upon the spirit of Mr. Nobel's interest in Stonehenge; hence the establishment of the Stonehenge Prize.

Sohlman went on to provide a brief explanation as to how the exclusive competition would unfold. Should information concerning Stonehenge emerge one day that he thought might be of interest to Lady Antrobus, it would be his pleasure to convey the relevant details. In the interim, using the same language found in his letters to the laureates, Sohlman concluded his letter by politely requesting that Lady Antrobus keep all matters related to the Stonehenge Prize strictly confidential.

Lady Antrobus was overjoyed. In thanking Sohlman for his welcome news, she included a copy of a guidebook that she had recently completed. Titled *A Sentimental and Practical Guide to Stonehenge*, the fifty-six-page pamphlet provided a concise yet comprehensive account of, in Lady

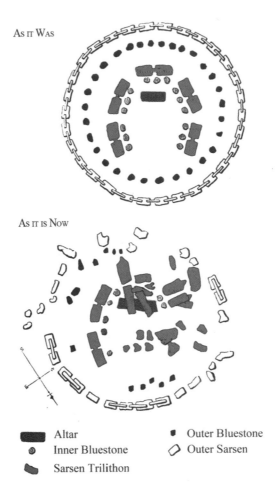

As it Was

As it is Now

Altar

Inner Bluestone

Sarsen Trilithon

Outer Bluestone

Outer Sarsen

Figure 16. The Lithology of Stonehenge.

A GREAT TRILITHON.

Figure 17. A Great Trilithon (top),
Stonehenge (bottom).

Antrobus's words, 'priceless Stonehenge.' On reading the dedication – 'For my friend Alfred Nobel' – Sohlman immediately purchased one hundred copies of the guidebook and ensured that each laureate received a copy with his or her invitation to compete for the Stonehenge Prize.

A Sentimental and Practical Guide to Stonehenge began with a succinct overview of the various theories addressing how Stonehenge had arisen, much as Lady Antrobus had earlier relayed to Nobel and Sohlman: Merlin's magic; the invading Romans and the Danes; and, of course, the Ancient Order of the Druids. To help 'poetically' describe the general architecture of Stonehenge, and its inherent beauty, Lady Antrobus included a number of photographs. There were also two helpful illustrations of the stone settings that contrasted Stonehenge 'As it Was' with Stonehenge 'As it Is Now.' As first erected, Stonehenge was presented as a design of four concentric stone circles surrounded by an earthwork – a shallow circular ditch. The outermost stone circle comprised large glacier-strewn sandstone boulders called 'sarsens.' Each sarsen was approximately sixteen feet in height and spanned by what was once a continuous ring of fitted lintels, or cross-beams. Slightly inside was a circle of much smaller 'bluestones,' each about six feet tall and named for their unusual blue colour when wet.

Further toward the centre of the monument was the most distinctive formation: a sarsen ring, drawn slightly apart to form a horseshoe, of five mammoth trilithons – independent three-stoned structures, each suggestive of a doorway. The largest of these stood twenty-four feet above the ground. A corresponding series of lesser bluestones represented the smallest, innermost circle. As depicted in the 'As it Is Now' illustration, however, many of the stones at Stonehenge were now fallen, broken, partially buried beneath the ground or – most commonly – absent altogether.

Lady Antrobus also described a number of other stones found within and outside the dominant structures: the crushed Altar Stone at the very centre of the ruins; the macabrely named Slaughter Stone half-submerged near an apparent entrance through the encircling earthwork, and furthest of all, the sixteen-foot-tall Heel Stone. There were also the two so-called Station Stones located near the edge of the earthwork's periphery.

In addition to the 'sentimental' impressions of Stonehenge that it contained, *A Sentimental and Practical Guide to Stonehenge* also incorporated certain 'practical' advice for those planning to visit Stonehenge. Sohlman hoped that such details might encourage prizewinners to travel to the site in order to conduct their own inspections and investigations. Hotels and inns in the medieval city of Salisbury and the village of Amesbury, the two closest communities to Stonehenge, were listed along with the tariff for rooms and meals. The White Hart in Salisbury, conveniently located near the cathedral, received the highest commendation. As Lady Antrobus noted, from there it was possible to travel to and from Stonehenge by way of Amesbury in a two-horse carriage for just one pound and ten shillings; an experienced driver was included in the cost. Wisely, Lady Antrobus chose not to include the following ancillary and disturbing detail: for two more shillings a day, guests could also hire out a hammer and chisel from the White Hart. It would appear that the hotel was still 'encouraging' those visiting Stonehenge to return from their outing with a small stone as souvenir.

PART THREE

THE MYSTERY OF STONEHENGE

CHAPTER 10

GREAT STONES
UNDERMINED BY WORMS

The first Nobel prizewinner to accept Sohlman's invitation was the Russian physiologist Ivan Petrovich Pavlov (1849–1936). In 1904 Pavlov had won the Nobel Prize in Medicine, 'in recognition of his work on the physiology of digestion, through which knowledge on vital aspects of the subject has been transformed and enlarged.' Through the novel use of various surgical techniques, Pavlov and his research assistants were able to study gastric and other digestive enzymes in dogs that were still able to eat and function normally following the operative procedures. Pavlov's key innovation was a delicate operation that fashioned an isolated pouch from a stomach that was otherwise left intact. This 'miniature' stomach still reacted to food that entered the larger stomach but its gastric secretions were uncontaminated by food and, as a result, could be measured easily. In subsequent studies Pavlov observed that a dog's salivary secretions could be elicited independently by the sound of a bell previously paired with the presentation of food. This was the 'conditioned' reflex, Pavlov's famous scientific legacy.

Pavlov's decision to respond to the Stonehenge challenge had little to do with an inherent interest in Stonehenge itself. In 1893, Nobel had sent an unsolicited letter to Pavlov. After confiding that he had endured years of ineffective treatment for chronic indigestion, Nobel asked Pavlov to set aside his experiments in dogs in order to study digestive problems in humans. Nobel then described specific experiments that Pavlov might wish to consider, including one proposal to transfuse suffering dyspeptics (like Nobel) with blood from giraffes or other healthy animals.[36] A 10,000-ruble donation accompanied the letter.

Pavlov, then overseeing a badly underfunded research program, was perplexed but grateful. The money was used to build a two-storey stone building, which featured a special operating facility on its second floor designed specifically for animals. In his letter of thanks to Nobel, Pavlov conveyed that, regrettably, he now restricted his physiologic experiments to dogs. Such subjects, he explained, were relatively inexpensive, easy to acquire and had a similar digestive system to that of humans. To demonstrate that he had not dismissed Nobel's imaginative notions out of hand, however, Pavlov reported that an experiment inspired by Nobel's suggestion – joining the circulatory systems of two dogs, one healthy, one not – had failed.

Pavlov ended his letter with a suggestion of his own that he hoped Nobel would find helpful. He had learned through his research that the personality and mood of a dog affected the production and flow of gastric secretions.[37]

---

36. As the world's tallest land animal, the giraffe's circulatory system featured a number of unique adaptations, such as unusually small red blood cells, that Nobel believed might be salubrious for humans. Nobel was likely also aware that giraffes (and other animals native to Africa) could then be found in the St. Petersburg zoo (in existence since 1865).

37. Freud was also keenly interested in the personality and mood of animals. He viewed dogs as particularly intuitive, and carefully observed his own dogs'

Pavlov therefore encouraged Nobel to set aside any worries while he ate so that the necessary 'appetite juices' could be produced. Some ten years later, Pavlov again acknowledged Nobel's considerable donation as well as his interest in the field of experimental physiology, this time in the lecture he delivered in Stockholm on receiving his Nobel Prize:

> *Some ten years ago, the great man to whom the annual science festival in Stockholm owes its existence honoured me and my friend, the late Professor Nencki, with a letter enclosing a considerable donation for the benefit of the laboratories under our direction. In that letter Alfred Nobel expressed his keen interest in physiological experiments and proposed that we should try several highly instructive projects.*

Later that same evening, an ebullient Pavlov also privately thanked those members of the Nobel family who attended the celebratory banquet.

Although Pavlov felt duty-bound to respond to Sohlman's invitation, by 1904 his work was confined exclusively to the physiology of animal digestion. As he was uncertain how his relatively narrow area of expertise might apply to Stonehenge, Pavlov consulted his wife Serafima Vasilievna Karchevskaya. It was his and Serafima's habit to take tea together after dinner, a time for reflection during which Pavlov and his wife would review with one another that day's accomplishments and challenges. It was Serafima,

---

reactions to each of his patients as they arrived for their analytic sessions (see Grinker, 1979). Jo-Fi, Freud's favourite Chow Chow, was the most empathic, although the dog had an unfortunate habit of aggressively sniffing his patients' genitals ('his' referring to Freud). Freud would later credit Jo-Fi as instrumental in alerting him to the construct of castration anxiety.

Figure 18. Ivan Pavlov.

for example, who had encouraged Pavlov to study dogs rather than cats, regarding the latter as ungrateful and spiteful animals.[38] Although Serafima thought her husband's loyalty to Nobel was misplaced, their discussion did lead to a fortuitous recollection.[39]

Years before, as an adolescent studying to be a priest in Ryazan, a provincial Russian village, Pavlov had come across a Russian translation of *On the Origin of Species*. The book, banned by his seminary, was a revelation. Inspired by the methodological rigour and vast objective data that Charles Darwin gathered to support his theories on evolution, Pavlov abruptly abandoned his religious training to study animal physiology at St. Petersburg University. He next completed medical school and further studies in medicine at St. Petersburg's Military Medical Academy, leaving the Academy in 1883. By then, Pavlov was fully proficient in English and had read all of Darwin's major texts, including Darwin's last substantive publication, a curious work titled *The Formation of Vegetable Mould, Through the Action of Worms, with Observations on Their Habits*, first published in 1881.

---

38. Serafima could also be spiteful and ungrateful. In the early years of the Nobel Banquet, it was the custom of Emanuel Nobel, Alfred Nobel's wealthy Russian nephew, to function as an ancillary host and to indulge all guests with champagne and caviar. Emanuel was delighted that Pavlov, a fellow countryman, had won a Nobel Prize and the two chatted together in Russian throughout the elaborate meal. As a result of their meeting, Pavlov deposited his entire Nobel Prize award (just over 73,000 gold rubles) in a St. Petersburg bank that Emanuel controlled, overriding Serafima's objections in the process. In 1917, the Bolsheviks confiscated the entire sum during the October Revolution. Within a year, Emanuel was forced to flee Russia for Sweden, a penniless exit similar to the one his grandfather Immanuel made some sixty years earlier. Thereafter, each 10th of December, a churlish Serafima bitterly reminded her husband of 'their' squandered fortune.

39. Is any recollection really fortuitous?

While sitting quietly with Serafima, Pavlov suddenly recalled that Darwin included field observations at Stonehenge within his treatise on the earthworm. It was Darwin's thesis that large stones such as those found at Stonehenge sink slowly downward into the ground due to the 'habits' of earthworms. As described by Darwin, the natural diet of an earthworm consists largely of half-decayed plant matter, much of it extracted from the soil it consumes while burrowing underground. The undigested material is eventually excreted through the worm's anus onto the soil's surface. Such depositions slowly accumulate to cover and, eventually, bury surface-lying objects. In the case of the large stones at Stonehenge, worms burrowing in the soil underneath the stones were forced to defecate just beyond the edge of each stone. Darwin therefore surmised that the ground abutting the stones must slowly rise while the stones themselves slowly sink due to this unceasing cycle of digestion and defecation.

The digestive process of an earthworm! Pavlov was now on comfortable intellectual terrain. Not only would he corroborate Darwin's thesis, he also intended to quantify the rate at which the stones were sinking into the earth. This, in turn, would allow him to project backwards in time and reliably determine when particular stones had toppled to the ground. Although Pavlov knew little more about Stonehenge than what he had read in *A Sentimental and Practical Guide to Stonehenge*, he trusted that such timelines would assist other enquirers with their investigations. He, in turn, would have the satisfaction of standing on Darwin's shoulders.

Mindful of the insistence on secrecy, Pavlov first corresponded with Sohlman to express his interest in the competition but also to learn whether Sohlman could assist with what might seem an unusual request. Sohlman was delighted with Pavlov's interest and forwarded his enquiry to an accommodating Lady Antrobus. Aided by the additional information and the earthworm-infested soil samples he subsequently received from Lady Antrobus, Pavlov's submission to Sohlman was dated 4 March 1906.[40] The short manuscript was written in Russian and accompanied by three illustrations. Two of these were hand-drawn by Pavlov. The third was the sketch Charles Darwin had made during his field trip to Stonehenge and published in *The Formation of Vegetable Mould, Through the Action of Worms, with Observations on Their Habits*. In order to include the appropriated figure with his submission, Pavlov had simply torn out the relevant illustration from his personal copy of Darwin's book.

---

40. At the conclusion of Pavlov's experiment, Serafima, always frugal, began to grow local potatoes and carrots in what remained of the soil that Lady Antrobus had sent to her husband. Serafima was to be impressed with how rapidly the vegetables grew in earth that had been well aerated by worms and informed her husband accordingly. Years later, the English author H. G. Wells visited Russia following World War I on hearing rumours that the Soviet Union's literary and scientific men were forced to work in deplorable conditions. In an article published in the *New York Times*, Wells commented on Pavlov's (transliterated as 'Pafloff' in the article) worm-littered laboratory, equating the lush growth of root vegetables there observed to that which might otherwise be found on a mid-west American farm.

(Translation)
Military Medical Academy, St. Petersburg

4 March 1906

Dear Mr. Ragnar Sohlman,

   In considering how to solve the mystery of Stonehenge, it seems prudent to begin with the words of the great Charles Darwin: 'At Stonehenge, some of the outer Druidical stones are now prostrate, having fallen at a remote but unknown period; and these have become buried to a moderate depth in the ground.'

   Darwin helpfully illustrated his observations as follows:

Fig. 7. Section through one of the fallen Druidical stones at Stonehenge, showing how much it had sunk into the ground. Scale ¼ in. to 1 ft.

   Declaring that such matters possess some interest, Darwin then established that the means by which such stones settle into the ground was due to the action of worms.

   It now may be of some merit to calculate the rate of such sinking, first turning to Darwin's own measurements. Darwin has written that he visited Stonehenge in 1877 and recorded the depths of three of the fallen stones, one of which – 17 feet long, 6 feet broad and 28½ inches thick – lay about 9½ inches beneath the level of the surrounding ground.

   With the generous assistance of Lady Antrobus, I have now learned that the stone in question toppled on 3 January 1797, its fall attributed to a day of severe frost followed by rapid thawing. As it required eighty years (that is, from 1797 to 1877) for the stone to sink to a depth of 9½ inches, one can calculate with some confidence that the stone settled at an average rate of approximately 0.12 of an inch per year.

In order to establish the generalizability of this rate of descent, I sought to determine whether similar findings could be elicited under experimental conditions. Lady Antrobus was again kind enough to assist, in this instance shipping to my laboratory in St. Petersburg three cubic metres of the chalky worm-infested soil she had excavated at Stonehenge, packed in well-moistened peat moss and topped by the downland grasses and flowers that characterize the Stonehenge landscape.

After ensuring that the worms – the British species *Lumbricus terrestris* – had survived their journey, I distributed the worm-infested soil in pots along with their native habitat. On top of the repotted soil I then distributed a layer of coal cinders; within two weeks I observed by naked eye the first of the worm excretions piled on the smaller of the cinder fragments.

After an interval of one year, a series of measurements were taken: the cinders were now consistently below the surface of the soil, at an average depth ascertained by caliper of between 0.11 and 0.13 inches. It will be apparent that these numbers obtained in vitro equate to those obtained in vivo above.

Having completed my calculations, I then felt it was incumbent upon me to dissect one of the worms and to conduct a microscopic examination of its internal anatomy.

The digestive contents were largely as anticipated: soil and semi-digested decaying plants and grasses within the worm's pharynx, oesophagus, crop and sand-filled gizzard. The material throughout the intestine and anus, now acted upon by various digestive enzymes, was of much finer consistency, except for the presence of well-preserved pollen grains, each 20 to 40 micrometres in size. (The surprising resiliency of the latter may prove to be of some import for those interested in the study of such fortitude.)

 In conclusion, I have calculated the annual rate at which a stone has settled into the ground since falling at Stonehenge in 1797. Similar rates of burial likely apply to other stones now prostrate at the site. To illustrate: by having an iron skewer driven into the ground, Lady Antrobus determined that a particularly well-buried stone, apparently of some size, lies approximately 4 feet below the surface. Assuming a settling of 0.12 inches per year, it can now be surmised that this stone fell 400 years ago. Although this does not resolve when the stone was erected, dating the past in this manner may help refine various historical events associated with both the destruction AND construction of Stonehenge.

 The accumulation of such observations may yet solve the mystery of Stonehenge.

With good wishes from St. Petersburg,
Ivan Petrovich Pavlov
Military Medical Academy, St. Petersburg

CHAPTER 11

WHEN STONEHENGE
WAS NEW

On 2 December 1907, Joseph 'Rudyard' Kipling evasively conveyed to a friend, 'We have to go abroad next week for a few days.' It was Kipling's discreet way of saying that he and his wife Carrie were off to Stockholm, where he was to accept the 1907 Nobel Prize for Literature. The award was 'in consideration of the power of observation, originality of imagination, virility of ideas and remarkable talent for narration that characterize the creations of this world-famous author.' Although only forty-one, Kipling's prodigious and diverse 'creations' already included novels such as *Captains Courageous* and *Kim*; numerous short story collections; poems by the hundreds; and, what was then an unusual genre for a 'serious' writer, morality tales for children, as found in the popular *Jungle Book* and *Just So* stories.

Kipling's literary talents had been recognized early. He was born in Bombay in 1865 to the artist John Lockwood Kipling, a curator at Lahore Museum, and his wife Alice. After spending an idyllic early childhood in the care of Hindu servants, Kipling – at just five years of age – was abruptly dispatched to England, along with his younger sister Twix, to receive a 'proper' education. For uncertain reasons, the two siblings were initially put in the care of foster parents (a couple called Holloway) in a small seaside town. It was an unfortunate decision, more so once Captain Holloway died. Thereafter, Mrs. Holloway and her adolescent son tyrannized Kipling (though they spared Twix), and it would not be until 1877 that Alice Kipling could return from India to rescue her son from the widow Holloway's authority.

Following his liberation, Kipling was boarded out at the United Services College in Devon, a relatively new school started by retired army officers. As most of the other students were either destined for careers in the army or were cast-offs from former schools, Kipling's writing talents stood out sharply from those of his peers. On graduation, Kipling returned to the Indian continent to begin his writing career as a precocious sixteen-year-old journalist. His father, who was aware of his son's literary skills but was unable to afford the tuition of an Oxford or Cambridge education, had secured a post for his son with the *Civil and Military Gazette*, an English newspaper based in Lahore. By the time Kipling returned to England seven years later, in 1889, compilations of his news stories were selling as paperbacks.

One of Kipling's new acquaintances in London was Wolcott Balestier, a charismatic American journalist and publishing agent. The two quickly became close friends and were in the midst of a writing collaboration, a novel entitled *The Naulahka*, when Balestier died suddenly of typhoid fever in December 1891. Within a month Kipling married Carrie, Wolcott's sister.[41] Carrie was helpfully protective of Kipling, but was not widely liked. Known as the 'hated wife,' she and Kipling spent the early years of their marriage in Vermont in a home on her family's estate. They were a family

41. Freud's concept of 'displacement' again appears to be relevant (see Footnote 23, p. 66.)

Figure 19. Rudyard Kipling.

of four when the Kiplings returned permanently to England in 1896. At the time of their crossing, Josephine Kipling was three and Elsie, her younger sister, was one. John, the youngest child, was born in August 1897.

Kipling initially revelled in his role as playful father. Tragically, Josephine Kipling contracted pneumonia on a family visit to America in 1899 and died at only six years of age. Three years later, the still-mourning family would retreat to Bateman's, a seventeenth-century house in rural East Sussex and Kipling's sanctuary over the next thirty-four years. Once Kipling was awarded the Nobel Prize, however, not even Bateman's isolated setting would protect the increasingly private writer from the onslaught of literary tourists he sought to avoid.

Unfortunately for the Kiplings, or at least Carrie, the 1907 Nobel ceremonies were unusually subdued. The King of Sweden had died on 8 December, just two days prior to the customary festivities. As the entire country was in mourning, Kipling was informed the banquet would be cancelled. As he would write Elsie and John later that day, 'At this news I looked properly grave and sad but I was very glad to escape from the speeches and banquet.'

After receiving his Nobel Prize, Kipling returned with Carrie briefly to Bateman's. The couple then departed with their children for a winter holiday in South Africa. It was shortly after the family's return from abroad in April 1908 that Kipling turned his attention to Stonehenge. On opening Sohlman's letter, which had arrived at Bateman's during his absence, Kipling had immediately announced to Carrie that he must see the great stones first hand if he were to solve their mystery. The decision was hardly startling: Kipling was enamoured with the history of England and had yet to visit Stonehenge. In truth, however, Kipling was just as motivated by the prospect of an outing in 'one of those motor-car things' as he was in solving the mystery of Stonehenge.

Kipling's mania for automobiles had begun in 1899. By 1900 he had purchased his first vehicle, an American-made steam car marketed as the Locomobile. Annoyed by the need to constantly refill its boiler, Kipling switched to the Lanchester, a British car with an internal combustion engine. After a second Lanchester proved as unreliable as the first, Kipling bought a German-built Daimler, which he named Gunhilda.[42] The car proved reasonably dependable and Kipling was genuinely delighted by the opportunity that a working car provided to explore the English countryside.

The distance from Bateman's to Stonehenge was 135 miles. If all went well, the trip could be accomplished in just over two days (Gunhilda was then achieving an impressive sixteen miles to the gallon). Based on the letter he wrote to his son John, then ten years old and at St. Aubyns boarding school in the town of nearby Rottingdean, it appeared Kipling still viewed Gunhilda as a capricious companion.

Bateman's
Burwash
Sussex.
Thursday 28 May 1908

My dear John:
It is a beastly drizzly morning. Breakfast was porridge, eggs and some awfully bad kippers and I am now up in

---

42. Kipling named almost all his cars. The Locomobile was 'the Holy Terror.' His first Lanchester was 'Number 16,' a reference to its production number off

my lonely study wishing you were here with me today. Mother and Elsie are already up to the village to spend your POOR father's money. At least Mother's cold is better – she was very tired yesterday and was resting most of the day.

If the weather warms, and it's not too wet, we will feed the new pigs after tea (those awful kippers). You will be surprised when you see them (the pigs that is).

You will be even more surprised to learn that Sunday next, Gunhilda, Baldwin and I leave for an adventure! It is a great SECRET so don't tell the other chaps. After motoring down to Rottingdean to see my dear old son, we are then off to see St__neh__nge!

It will be a twisty-twirly journey that looks like this:

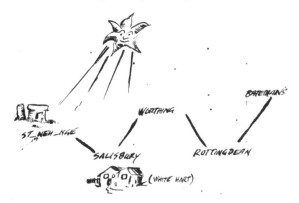

If we can avoid the dogs, and if Gunhilda be-haves (unberufen!), we just might make our destination. Have you heard of S__one__enge before? It is an old temple made of stones. I plan to send you one as a keepsake. And

the assembly line, while his second Lanchester was 'Jane Cakebread' after a London woman infamous for her disorderly intemperance.

I'll have a story to tell you on my return. That is if I leave at all – the real adventure is Gunhilda.

Now – I have other letters and letters to write (but none more pleasing than this).

Mother sends heaps of love and hopes you are behaving decently.

Meantime I am

Your affectionate
Dadd-o!

Did I tell you how very pleased I am that you are taking more interest in your Greek?

Baldwin was a reference to Kipling's chauffeur (and servant) at the time. Though Kipling loved motoring, he never actually drove. He did, however, take his role as navigator seriously. Based on the map Kipling drew, the circuitous trip to Stonehenge would – after visiting John in Rottingdean – include two overnight stops, first in Worthing and then in Salisbury. At the latter destination, it appears Kipling planned to stay at the White Hart, presumably on the basis of the recommendation in Lady Antrobus' guidebook. It was then a short ten miles to Stonehenge, by way of a winding dirt road that trailed the banks of the River Avon.

Of note, Kipling – already weary of his role as a public figure – had chosen not to inform Lady Antrobus of his pending visit. Wearing a large hat and oversized coat, he went unrecognized, as he intended, at Stonehenge. Just 5 feet 6 inches tall and handicapped by his severe short-sightedness, Kipling was forced to inspect each stone with his nose virtually pressed up against its surface. Despite this inconvenience, Kipling persevered for the greater part of a day in order to complete his detailed observations.

After returning to Bateman's, Kipling turned to the challenge at hand. Assisting Kipling would be Puck, a playful fairy in English folklore and a well-known character due to his presence in Shakespeare's popular play *A Midsummer Night's Dream*. Kipling had first presented Puck to his readers in 1906 in a volume titled *Puck of Pook's Hill*. The book was a collection of stories in which Puck introduces two children, Dan and his younger sister Una, to selected events of old English history. Kipling apparently viewed the literary form as a playful and perfect vehicle to address the mystery of how Stonehenge came to be. As was Kipling's practice, an imaginative drawing accompanied his submission. Perhaps suspecting that the nature of his 'solution' might not be immediately obvious, Kipling also included the following short letter addressed to Sohlman:

Bateman's, / Burwash, / Sussex. / 26 June 1908.

Dear Mr. Sohlman,

I am now responding with my 'solution' to the mystery of Stonehenge. I have used Mr. Nobel's very trick: to provoke the interest of others in solving the mystery of Stonehenge.

But you'll soon see my cleverness. Whereas Mr. Nobel has turned to grown-ups for assistance, I have turned to those much wiser — our beloved children.

Ever sincerely,
Rudyard Kipling

When Stonehenge Was New

It was mid-afternoon at Stonehenge. Dan and Una had walked the two miles from their home in Amesbury to be amongst the stones. It was their favourite place to play – stones to leap over and dart in between and best of all, to hide behind. After three games of hide-and-seek – Una was pleased as she had spied Dan straight away each time! – the children were hungry.

It was Una who spread their food on their special picnic table – a large, flat stone a little away from the rest. After eating mother's hard-boiled eggs and biscuits, Dan and Una stretched out comfortably atop their stone table and were soon sleeping under the drowsy late-afternoon sun. It was a loud clatter from behind the tallest stone that woke them.

From the very-same spot where Dan had tried to hide from Una, out jumped a tiny, pointy-eared person with a not-so-tiny grin. With a bow and a tip of his cloth cap, he demanded: 'What young visitors have we sleeping here?'

Dan and Una gasped, each too scared to answer.

'By Oak, Ash and Thorn!' Puck cried, in his deepest voice. 'Who sleeps amongst the stones?' he demanded again, now trying to look fierce.

'Who are you?' stammered Dan, finally. He was standing in front of Una, trying to be brave.

Puck smiled. 'I'm Puck, the oldest Old Thing in England.'

The children stared in silence – they had never seen anyone like Puck before. He had no shoes on his hairy feet and six points on his cap. There wasn't much in between –Puck was as small as he was peculiar.

'Please don't stare,' said Puck, jumping on top of their stone table. 'Have you never met a fairy person before?'

It was Una who spoke, not quite so frightened as she had been. She was taller than Puck, or would be if she were to stand on her tiptoes.

'We were always told by Mother and Father that fairies were make-believe,' Una said as politely and bravely as she could.

'Make-believe!' Puck thumped his chest and tried to look angry. And then he laughed. 'It's all right,' he said, and added, 'I know many don't believe, at least not until they see me!' Puck laughed again.

'Are you very old?' asked Una.

'As old as the stones,' said Puck. 'Good people of this land used to set my dish of cream for me o' nights when Stonehenge was new. It was different here then.'

'How?' asked Una, even braver now.

Puck pointed to the grass-clothed downs that surrounded the stones. 'It was forest in those days, with great oak trees. And all the stones were greater still – tall, and straight.' Puck looked up at the stones that still towered above them. 'Why here stood the greatest Temple of the Druids.'

'The Druids?' asked Una.

'Wise men with wild beards and long white cloaks,' said Puck. 'They were healers with magic potions, sorcerer–priests with the gift of prophecy. It was the Druids who prayed to the gods, begging them to protect their people. But the gods wanted something terrible in return.'

'Was it people burned in wicker baskets?' asked Dan. 'Like teacher taught us in school?'

Una shut her eyes and shuddered.

'Yes,' said Puck. 'A wicker basket in the shape of a man, but bigger, and, inside the wicker basket, fair maidens, tied and burned alive.'

'Little children too, said teacher,' added Dan, solemnly.

Puck nodded, just as gravely.

Una was now very scared. 'But why, Puck?' she asked.

'To please their Gods. So that battles would be won and the sick would be healed. So that the sun would rise in the sky and the moon and the stars would light their nights.'

'Was it the Druids who brought the stones here to Amesbury?' asked Dan. 'Was it their magic that did it?'

'It must have been magic,' said Puck, 'magic more powerful and black than a thousand Merlins could conjure. But I was a wee thing then and did not see it done. Not even I know the story of the stones,' said Puck.

'Would the Druids not tell?' asked Una.

'No, never,' said Puck. 'They would keep the secrets of the stones though they were tied and burned alive.'

'Are there Druids still about, Puck?' shivered Una.

'Most of them are gone now,' said Puck, 'but some hid in the far-far-away forests, and wait there still, to return again one day. It is here at Stonehenge that their magic is strongest. It is said that when they are once again at Stonehenge, the Druids will set the fallen stones up straight as first they were and put right the missing stones.'

'What made the Druids go away?' Dan asked.

'It was the Romans,' said Puck. 'By sword and by arrow they were conquered.'

'I know who the Romans were!' said Dan. 'Soldiers dressed in steel led by Caesar, the mightiest soldier of them all.'

'Good lad,' said Puck. 'When the Druids return, and if you are as brave as Caesar, you can hide and watch the Druids work their magic. And you will learn the mystery as to how the stones came to be at Amesbury and how they stand so tall!'

'I will do it!' said Dan. 'Una, will you hide with me? Together we can watch the Druids make Stonehenge new again!'

Una was silent. She looked at Puck.

'But if the Druids come back, Puck, will it be safe to be at Stonehenge?' Una was scared again.

Puck thought before he answered. Taking a small knife from his belt, Puck began to carve the image of a short-hilted dagger with a triangular blade on the largest of the stones.

'What's that for?' asked Una.

'It is the knife of the Druids,' Puck answered, 'for when they cut the sacred mistletoe.' Puck hesitated, and then he added, 'And for other things too.'

'What other things?' asked Una.

Puck paused. It was a minute more before he continued. 'To cut the throats of two white bulls, when the moon is full,' he said quietly.

'And other things too?' asked Dan.

Puck nodded and the children were silent.

Puck finished the carving of the dagger. 'This is a dagger that only the Druids can see. And now you. Those who can see the dagger need not fear the Druids.'

Puck's voice was now strong and reassuring. 'You will be safe. And one day, when the Druids return, you will hide and learn their secrets, and together you will solve the mystery of Stonehenge.'

By then it had grown cool and the shadows were growing.

It was time to return home.

Puck gave Una and Dan each three leaves – one of Oak, one of Ash, one of Thorn.

'Bite these,' said Puck as the three walked hand-in-hand back toward Amesbury, 'so that what you've seen and heard is yours alone. You will forget meeting me here today, but you will always be able to see the knife of the Druids. Keep it your secret.'

The children bit hard.

The old stones, now almost black, faded into darkness.

THE END

CHAPTER 12

SEABORNE STONES

Theodore Roosevelt's lecture for his Nobel Prize for Peace was delivered in the National Theatre in Kristiania, Norway, on 5 May 1910. The prize had been awarded in 1906 for the role he played in ending the hostilities between Russia and Japan (the Russo–Japanese War) the previous year. As the 26th President of the United States, Roosevelt had overseen weeks of difficult negotiations between the two warring parties. Despite mediating a successful outcome – the Treaty of Portsmouth – a Peace Prize for Roosevelt was even then a controversial accolade. Although he espoused talking softly, Roosevelt's real pleasure came from brandishing a blustering imperialist's stick; it was Roosevelt's assemblage of battleships offshore the isthmus of Panama, so-called 'gunboat diplomacy,' that had 'encouraged' Latin America to permit the United States to begin construction of the Panama Canal.

Roosevelt had delayed his trip to Kristiania until 1910 as he had felt it improper to receive the honour in the midst of his presidential duties.[44] Directly following the end of

44. Such a delayed Nobel Lecture is now discouraged. According to the statutes of the Nobel Foundation, 'It shall be incumbent on a prizewinner, whenever this is possible, to give a lecture on a subject relevant to the work for which the prize has been awarded. Such a lecture should be given before, or no later than six months after, the Festival Day in Stockholm or, in the case of the Peace

his second presidential term, Roosevelt left for a year-long safari in East Africa, landing first in Mombasa, then the capital city of the British East Africa Protectorate, in April 1909. By the time Roosevelt arrived in Norway by way of Khartoum, he and his middle son Kermit had slaughtered over 11,000 animals, including six rare white rhinoceroses. Though the entire expedition was little more than a well-orchestrated bloodbath, over 2,000 Norwegians politely applauded the big-game hunter as he lectured on the international use of arbitration.

Among those whom Roosevelt invited to join him in a private audience following his Nobel Lecture was Ragnar Sohlman.[45] As Roosevelt was no longer encumbered with his presidential responsibilities, he had asked Sohlman to travel to Kristiania so that he could reconsider whether to challenge for the Stonehenge Prize. Sohlman's personal petition was apparently convincing. By chance, Roosevelt was next scheduled to deliver a number of lectures in Britain, including the prestigious Romanes Lecture at Oxford University. Roosevelt altered his British itinerary and arranged to add a day trip to Stonehenge. At Roosevelt's request, Sohlman contacted Lady Antrobus and a discreet and private tour for an 'illustrious American visitor' was arranged. Before returning to America,

---

Prize, in Oslo.' The Festival Day is a reference to 10 December, the anniversary of Nobel's death and the date on which the Nobel Prizes are awarded (almost always in person) to each prizewinner.

45. Roosevelt also received members of the Norges Jeger-og Fiskerforbun (the Norwegian Association of Hunters and Anglers) and immediately accepted their invitation to join a hunting expedition to Helgeland in the northern part of the country. Before leaving Norway, Roosevelt and Kermit had substantially contributed to the extinction of that country's wild boar (*Sus scrofa*) and the European bison (*Bison bonasus*).

Figure 20. Theodore Roosevelt.

Roosevelt had not only toured Stonehenge but had queried Lady Antrobus on its origins, conducted his own historical research, and had a plan of action in mind.[46]

Impressed by the scale of leadership and organization that such a strategic campaign would have entailed, Roosevelt was intrigued by how the giant stones had arrived at Stonehenge. The source of the largest of these – the sarsens – had been convincingly localized to the nearby Marlborough Downs where sarsen outcrops were still found at the time of Roosevelt's visit. Though the tallest sarsen at Stonehenge weighed over forty tons, it was generally agreed that the sarsens had been sledge-hauled over the roughly twenty-four miles from the Marlborough Downs to the Stonehenge site, tipped into holes of a sufficient depth and pulled upright by hauling ropes. It was how the smaller of the stones – the bluestones – had arrived at Stonehenge that had remained so puzzling. Though dwarfed by the sarsens, the bluestones were still of substantial size: up to eight feet in height and four to five tons apiece. Despite careful petrological surveys, no additional rock specimens identical to bluestones could be found in the immediate vicinity of Stonehenge. This meant, as the only reasonable explanation, that the bluestones must have been moved over a great distance, yet no one had convincingly explained from where and in what manner.

To solve this mystery, Roosevelt's bold notion was to prove that a bluestone could be transported from Ireland to Stonehenge relying on only those techniques and conveyances as would have been accessible to the original

46. The initials T. R. are still visible on one of the outer sarsens (stone No. 7 according to Professor Flinders Petrie's numbering plan of 1880).

builders. Roosevelt had settled upon Ireland as the source of the bluestones on the basis of a literal reading of one of the earliest known accounts of Stonehenge's origin. In 1138 CE, Geoffrey of Monmouth wrote in *Historia Regum Britanniae* (*The History of the Kings of Britain*) that King Aurelius, an important monarch in fifth-century Britain, had resolved to commemorate the Saxon slaughter of 460 of his kingdom's unarmed earls and noblemen near Amesbury. As recounted by Geoffrey, the king's advisor, Merlin the Wizard, counselled the king to 'Send for the *Giant's Dance*,' a reference to a giant ring of stones situated on Mount Killaraus in Ireland. With Merlin's assistance, the stones were magically dismantled and transported by sail to Stonehenge where they were re-erected to stand as an enduring monument to those massacred.

Advising Roosevelt on his plan was Robert E. Peary, the celebrated American Arctic explorer. In 1894, after hearing rumours of an 'iron mountain,' Peary and an Eskimo guide successfully located three enormous iron meteorites thirty-five miles from the community of Cape York in northern Greenland. Peary immediately resolved to transport the meteorites back to New York City. After several failed attempts, the meteorites were ultimately secured to timber planks and slowly pushed over rollers to the coastline. There, with the assistance of a ship-to-shore trolley, winches, lines and an improvised ice floe as a 'ferryboat,' each of the meteorites was safely moved onto a waiting ship. The *Ahnighoto*, weighing more than thirty-one tons and the last and largest of the meteorites to be removed, finally arrived at the Brooklyn Naval Yard on 2 October 1896.

Figure 21. Robert Peary.

Roosevelt was aware of Peary's exploits. Years earlier he had written a positive review of Peary's *Northward Over the 'Great Ice,'* a self-aggrandizing memoir in which Peary had included a melodramatic account of the meteorites' removal.[47] Recognizing that Peary's hard-learned lessons would be a valuable and relevant asset in his effort to duplicate the original journey of the bluestones, Roosevelt invited the now-retired rear admiral to help design the anticipated venture.

The two men strategized at Roosevelt's home on Long Island throughout the summer of 1910. It was Roosevelt who insisted that the expedition begin from Kildare, a small inland county west of Dublin. In Geoffrey's account, the source of the bluestones was Ireland's Mount Killaraus. As no mountain by that name was known in Ireland, most reputable historians had dismissed Mount Killaraus as mythical. Roosevelt, however, was convinced Killaraus was a misspelling for Kildare, whose terrain, if not quite mountainous, did at least feature a number of prominent hills. There was one other intriguing detail influencing Roosevelt's decision. He had learned that large ancient quartz boulders were strewn throughout County Kildare; some of these were still clustered suggestively in circles reminiscent of those found at Stonehenge.

---

47. Peary was not entirely forthcoming in his memoir. One of the unreported difficulties of the trans-Atlantic crossing of the *Ahnighoto* was due to Peary's failure to appreciate the strong magnetic pull of the iron meteorite. This magnetic field disabled the ship's compass, which unwaveringly pointed to the ship's hold where the meteorite had been lowered regardless of which direction the ship was actually heading. It was not until Peary recognized the northern tip of Baffin Island that he realized how far north he had veered. Forced to rely on a sextant and outdated methods of celestial navigation, Peary finally arrived in Brooklyn a concerning three months overdue.

As for the details of the journey itself, Roosevelt deferred to Peary's greater experience. The initial overland portion would be accomplished by means of sledges on timber rollers that were to be steered by cattle-hide guide ropes. Based on his Arctic explorations, Peary advised that vats of animal fat must also be available to ensure the guide ropes were kept malleable and waterproof. In the absence of a locally sourced bluestone, Roosevelt had already obtained permission from the Kildare County Council to transport one of the sizeable quartz boulders, in the four-to-five-ton range, referred to above. It seemed reasonable, to Roosevelt at least, that a boulder of similar size and shape to a bluestone might serve as a realistic substitute.

Once the 'bluestone' was rolled to the Irish shoreline, the dangerous journey by water would then begin. Peary again drew from his experiences with the Eskimos. First, the 'bluestone' would be secured aboard a twenty-foot-square raft lashed between two primitive canoe-like vessels. It would then be rowed across the treacherous Irish Sea using the prevailing winds and the shortest route possible. On reaching the Welsh shoreline, the raft would travel up the Bristol Channel and then inland via a connected series of navigable streams and rivers. The last of these, the River Avon, flowed to within two miles of Stonehenge.

Roosevelt's submission was dated 1 September 1910.[48]

---

48. By then, the Roosevelt–Peary collaboration had ended poorly. There are two versions to the story. In one, Peary is said to have resigned his commission when Roosevelt refused to support his plan to transport a dismantled Stonehenge back to New York City. The other account has Peary quitting on learning Roosevelt intended to relegate him from the rank of expedition co-commander to steward, a role limited to overseeing the crew's daily rations. Freud's construct of sibling rivalry would, of course, nicely account for Peary's humiliating demotion.

Under separate cover, he addressed a number of practical considerations. To adequately finance the proposed expedition, Roosevelt planned to seek funds from the American Museum of Natural History. He would offer the New York–based museum the exclusive right to permanently display the expedition's raft and sleds in exchange for 10,000 American dollars. As for Roosevelt's crew, these would be small-statured[49] recruits from the Rough Riders, his loyal volunteer regiment that had courageously charged up the San Juan Hill in Cuba under his command during the Spanish–American War. If there was strenuous adventure to be found in solving the mystery of Stonehenge, Roosevelt was the man to seize upon it.

49. Roosevelt had read that prehistoric men were rarely more than 5 foot 6 inches tall.

August 27, 1910

My dear Mr. Sohlman,

Thank you again for agreeing to meet with me at such short notice. As I explained in Kristiania, it was not possible for me to initially accept your kind invitation of some years ago. Now, however, I am at last free of my presidential duties. It will therefore be my pleasure to address Alfred Nobel's intriguing challenge – that is, to solve the mystery of Stonehenge.

To begin:

Legend points to the wild home of the bluestones as Mount Killaraus in Ireland. Though some believe their arrival at Stonehenge is only explicable by the powers of Merlin, I now propose a more prosaic explanation. Further, I intend to establish the veracity of this explanation and thereby address one of the mysteries of Stonehenge.

Let us agree:

It is certain that the builders of Stonehenge would wish to transport the bluestones from Mount Killaraus where possible by water, as this would allow a substantial reduction in time and man-power.

What then is the most likely manner in which the transport of the bluestones from Mount Killaraus to Stonehenge occurred?

The first stage of such a journey begins on the slopes of Mount Killaraus (now spelled Kildare). From these outcrops, let us again agree that sledges hauled the stones by the shortest route to the coast. From there, the next and most dangerous stage of the journey begins – crossing the Irish Sea. It is the practicability of this crossing that I wish to demonstrate by employing only those same primitive methods available to those who built Stonehenge.

First, a square raft of suitable logs consisting of two layers lashed together at right angles will be built. The raft will then be strapped between two dug-outs, each hollowed from a large Irish tree trunk split longitudinally. A stone between four and five tons will then be lowered onto the raft. Once the minimum sizes of the various sea-craft and the number of crew required are determined in practical trials, the sea journey will be undertaken.

I have plotted the route for the transport of the bluestones on the map that accompanies this correspondence.

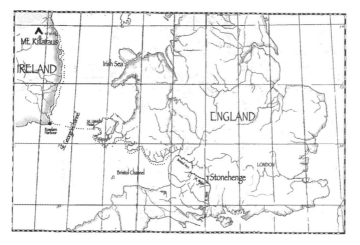

After considering the sequence of high and low water at suitable landing distances, tidal patterns, water hazards, tidal streams and prevailing wind conditions, I have determined it is wisest to first travel south along the Irish coast. On reaching Rosslare Harbor, it is then east across the Irish Sea to St. David's Head in Wales, a distance of 47 miles as the great American eagle flies.

The greatest challenge of the journey now over, it is then a matter of hugging the shores of South Wales while travelling laterally in the Bristol Channel. On reaching the lower estuary of the River Severn at Avonmouth, we will then continue inland by way of three small rivers – the Bristol Avon, the Frome, the Wylye – and two trifling portages. We find the River Avon at Salisbury. It is then upstream just past Amesbury, and a final two miles by sledge to Stonehenge.

There are admittedly a number of dangers inherent in such a journey. The timid will most fear the ferocious tides in the St. George's Channel and the Bitches Tidal Rapid as one approaches St. David's Head. Yet with our predicted paddling speed of 4.5 knots, and the patience to await a neap tide and settled weather, it will be Ireland at dawn and Wales at dusk. Should there be rough weather in the Bristol Channel, the shores of South Wales afford numerous protected beaches where one can outwait it.

Such an experiment will answer the questions by what route, and by what means, the bluestones were transported to Stonehenge. But why the stones were moved must remain a mystery for others to solve.

Sincerely,
Theodore Roosevelt

CHAPTER 13

THE CURVE OF KNOWNS

Three individuals shared the 1903 Nobel Prize in Physics. One half of the prize was awarded to Professor Henri Becquerel for his discovery of spontaneous radioactivity. The other half was jointly awarded to Marie and Pierre Curie, 'in recognition of the extraordinary services they have rendered by their joint researches on the radiation phenomena discovered by Professor Henri Becquerel.' Inspired by Becquerel's observation that uranium salts emitted a new form of radiation, the Curies had detected that pitchblende, an oxide of uranium, emitted an even more powerful form of these mysterious rays, an energy force Marie named radioactivity. On the assumption that unknown chemical elements must account for these more potent rays, the Curies eventually isolated two new highly radioactive substances they named radium and polonium.

The Curies' discoveries were extraordinary achievements, all the more so for Marie Curie's early life circumstances. Born Maria Salomea Sklodowska in 1867, she had grown up as the youngest of five children in Warsaw, Poland, a city then under the repressive occupation of Tsarist Russia. Her childhood and early adolescent years, characterized by significant financial hardships, were further tested by the deaths of her mother and a sister. Despite these misfortunes, Maria graduated from her gymnasium at just fifteen years of age. As Polish universities were then reserved exclusively for men, Maria had little choice but to work as a governess in a small Polish village. The money she earned was used to fund her older sister Bronia's medical studies in Paris. Once Bronia was established as a physician, the sisters had agreed that it would then be Maria's turn to be supported by Bronia. Using the French version of her name, 'Marie' finally enrolled at the Sorbonne in 1891 and, with Bronia's help, managed to excel in her studies while subsisting in a tiny attic room on a budget of three francs per day.

In 1895, after a short courtship, Marie married Pierre Curie, a physicist then employed as an instructor at a new technical school in Paris. The newlyweds settled in Paris and lived frugally as they pursued their joint efforts to purify radium and polonium, the topic of Marie's doctoral thesis. Their makeshift laboratory, supplied with only the most primitive equipment, was a small, unheated storage shed. The Curies would eventually detect minuscule amounts of purified radium after four years of relentless, physically demanding work. To celebrate their momentous discovery, the couple would return to their laboratory in the evenings and – naive to the dangers – bask romantically in the strange blue luminescence of a highly radioactive material.

After winning the Nobel Prize in 1903, the Curies continued to live modestly despite the opportunities afforded by their newfound celebrity and wealth. On discovering radium, Marie and Pierre had chosen to publish their technical data related to radium's isolation and purification, thereby forgoing lucrative patents on the manufacturing process. The same altruistic spirit would guide the relatively rapid exhaustion

Figure 22. Marie Curie.

of the couple's Nobel Prize money.[50] Instead of the lifetime of financial independence accrued to most other Nobel prizewinners, the Curie household remained dependent on their modest teaching salaries. Yet the Curies were content with their unassuming lifestyle and their growing family. In December 1904, Marie gave birth to Eve, her second daughter; Irene, the Curies' first child, was then seven years old.

In June 1905, the Curies belatedly visited Stockholm to deliver the obligatory Nobel Lecture. Pierre, who spoke on behalf of himself and his wife, seemed to delight in his continuous references to the contributions of 'Mme. Curie.' The lecture ended with an analogy to Nobel's discovery of explosives:

> *It can even be thought that radium could become very dangerous in criminal hands, and here the question can be raised whether mankind benefits from knowing the secrets of Nature, whether it is ready to profit from it or whether this knowledge will not be harmful for it. The example of the discoveries of Nobel is characteristic, as powerful explosives have enabled man to do wonderful work. They are also a terrible means of destruction in the hands of great criminals who are leading the peoples toward war. I am one of those who believe with Nobel that mankind will derive more good than harm from the new discoveries.*

It was prescient and poignant rhetoric. At the time of delivering the Nobel Lecture, Pierre was already experiencing

---

50. The disbursements included salaries for lab assistants, scholarships for Polish students, and – most notably – payments toward the prohibitive costs of producing radium and other radioactive elements. The one personal indulgence the Curies allowed themselves was the domestic installation of indoor plumbing.

bouts of crippling pain and unexplained paresthesia in his fingertips, the debilitating effects of what would now be immediately recognized as the symptoms of early radiation poisoning.

Less than one year later, the Curies' comfortable partnership was ended by tragedy. On 19 April 1906, Pierre was crushed by a horse-drawn wagon while walking distractedly across the Rue Dauphiné on a rainy Parisian day. Despite frantic efforts by horrified bystanders to resuscitate Pierre, he died almost instantly. A devastated Marie was now a single parent, overwhelmed and depressed. With the assistance of her widowed father-in-law and a series of Polish governesses, Marie initially managed to care for the children and continue with her research and teaching responsibilities. But with her father-in-law's death in February 1910, and the loss of the emotional stability he had brought to the household, Marie was left disconsolate and alone. For comfort, she turned to Paul Langevin, a distinguished physicist who had been a friend and colleague to both Marie and Pierre. Within months, the two became lovers and secretly rented a small apartment to accommodate their trysts.

There was one significant complication. Langevin was an unhappily married father of four young children. During the Easter holidays of 1911, Marie and Paul's pied-à-terre was burglarised and their intimate love letters were stolen. A furious and jealous Madame Langevin had helped orchestrate the theft and, within days, she was threatening to disclose the letters publicly. A series of attacks on Marie's character followed, and the scandal became a *cause célèbre* in Paris's leading newspapers. Fairly or unfairly, Madame Langevin was represented as the defenceless and undeserving victim, while Marie Curie was depicted as the *femme fatale.* Threats of a public trial over custody of the children quickly ensued. Although Marie's financial situation was already tenuous, in August 1911 she made a number of significant 'loans' to Langevin on the pretence that they were 'to pay life insurance,' a euphemism for blackmail payments that the aggrieved Madame Langevin was demanding from her husband.

Curie was now financially desperate. The 'loans' had depleted all funds associated with the 1903 Nobel Prize. Fearing further extortion, Curie reluctantly turned to Sohlman's curious invitation of some years earlier. Then, the opportunity for her and her husband to compete for the Stonehenge Prize was dismissed as a frivolous distraction; now, however, a significant monetary award associated with solving the mystery of Stonehenge could be her salvation. Focused and distressed, the submission she forwarded to Sohlman was dated 10 September 1911, just three months before the competition for the Stonehenge Prize was to close officially.[51]

Ironically, on 7 November 1911, Curie received a telegram from Carl Aurivillius, secretary to the Royal Swedish Academy of Sciences. Unexpectedly, Curie learned she was to receive the 1911 Nobel Prize for Chemistry, 'in recognition of her services to the advancement of chemistry by the discovery of the elements radium and polonium, by the isolation of radium and the study of the nature and compounds of this remarkable element.' It was the first time that a second Nobel Prize had been awarded to an earlier prizewinner.

---

51. Unknown to Curie (and initially to this author, see Appendix II), her submission for the Stonehenge Prize, like virtually every other document written in her contaminated laboratory, was covered with radioactive dust.

FACULTÉ DES SCIENCES DE PARIS

12, Rue Cuvier

LABORATOIRE   *Paris,*

de   *le Septembre 10, 1911*

PHYSIQUE GENERALE

Dear Monsieur Sohlman,

Forgive this rather belated response but I wish to address a challenge you posed some time ago.

In the Nobel Lecture delivered by my late husband, we posited that radioactive phenomena could also prove important in disciplines other than the fields of physics and chemistry. A striking application now being studied by colleagues is the possible use of radium rays in the successful treatment of certain diseases. Not yet considered, however, is the role that radio-elements might yet play in the field of archaeological science. I now suggest that such considerations may meaningfully contribute to solving the mystery of Stonehenge.

The starting point of the argument is as follows: We know that radioactive elements constitute continuous sources of energy and disintegrate spontaneously. What is remarkable about such disintegration is that the absolute immutability of chemical elements no longer holds true. Radioactive substances give birth to a train of atoms of lesser and lesser weights, achieving stability only when the derived substance attains an inactive state. It follows that a greater proportion of such disintegration products should be found as geological formations increase in age.

In less hypothetical terms, it seems to have been proved (by Rutherford) that when considering the derivative products of radioactive uranium, the final product is nothing more than lead. Increases in the amount of lead, relative to uranium, should therefore occur as the age of the uranium–ore increases. The application of this relationship is relatively simple. Boltwood and others have already measured such lead–uranium ratios, with the result that geological time has been extended far beyond that previously appreciated.

This is not all.

CONSIDER that radioactive elements are found not just in geological formations but also in living things or things that were ONCE living – items such as fragments of ancient bone, or the charcoal ashes of ancient wood fires.

Now also consider that each radioactive element demonstrates a regularity of decay, each according to a characteristic time constant. It can now be stated that the emanation from polonium diminishes roughly by one-half in a period of 140 days, and that from radium by one-half every 2,600 years. It is anticipated that half-lives of other known radioactive elements, such as actinium, will soon be established – ranging from fractions of a second to millions of years.

SUPPOSE now that one could identify a radioactive element that is absorbed in living tissue and ceases to be absorbed at the time the organism dies. It will be apparent that once death occurs, the quantity of the radioactive element within the tissue should begin to decrease according to its characteristic time constant.

ASSUME therefore that one can identify and measure such a radioactive element in archaeological samples for which the historical age is known by other means — such as ancient trees whose ages can otherwise be ascertained by tree-ring dating or those wooden artefacts whose ages can be derived from the written historical records of ancient literate civilizations.

It follows that a series of radioactive measurements can then be plotted, each against the historical age of its source. It is suggested that such a CURVE OF KNOWNS could begin with wood samples from the First Dynasty tombs of the Egyptian kings at Saqqara — roughly 5,000 years old and the earliest historical date of any certainty. As one draws closer to the present time, I am told that an increasing range of samples becomes available: wood from an Egyptian pyramid, a tomb and a funeral ship; the stump of an ancient California redwood tree; and buried bread charred by the volcanic eruption of Pompeii.

The Figure that follows shows the construction of the projected Curve of Knowns. It now only remains to obtain the relevant sample from Stonehenge, to measure the remaining quantity of the radioactive element in question, and to cross-date that measurement onto the Curve of Knowns. Consider, for example, if cremated human bones had been scattered at the time Stonehenge was erected. The radioactive study of such ancient organic materials might one day yield an approximate date for the period in which the large stones were raised and hence a clearer sense of EXACTLY when Stonehenge was built, and by extension, by whom.

In such a manner, radioactive decay becomes a fore-seeable means for dating not just Stonehenge but, in more general terms, for investigating the history of humankind.

If such a supposition is found to be worthy of the prize, I would appreciate if a money transfer could be effected immediately to the following bank:

Société Générale S. A.

29 Boulevard Haussmann

Paris

Regretfully, should it prove necessary to give a lecture relevant to this work, ill health and the demands of two children preclude travel to Sweden in the foreseeable future.

Respectfully,
M. Curie

Note – It is a pleasure to acknowledge the Société des Antiquaires de France, whose members helpfully proposed the historical items and their ages to include in the Curve of Knowns.

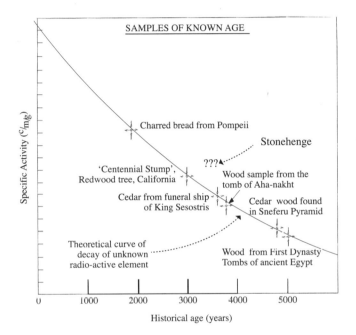

CURVE OF KNOWNS

PART FOUR

DELIBERATIONS

CHAPTER 14

10 DECEMBER 1911

In the end, of the sixty Nobel Laureates contacted by Sohlman, it was only Pavlov, Kipling, Roosevelt and Curie who submitted entries for the Stonehenge Prize.[52] Sohlman was disappointed but not terribly surprised. As a new focus of serious enquiry, Stonehenge would have represented a radical departure for each laureate he had contacted over the preceding decade. Moreover, the monetary value of the prize – 60,000 Swedish kronor – was substantial, but apparently too little an incentive to motivate those already allotted a lucrative Nobel Prize. Most laureates, of course, were otherwise occupied with long-defined interests of their own choosing. There were likely other considerations that accounted for their collective disinterest. Many prizewinners may have feared tarnishing their reputations by participating in a curious competition; others may have dreaded failing to meet the burdensome expectations now attached to even the most innocuous of their post Nobel Prize intellectual pursuits.

---

52. The number, sixty, was greater than might be expected (i.e., fifty based on five Nobel Prizes per year for a ten-year period) as it was not uncommon for a Nobel Prize to be awarded to more than one recipient. It should also be noted that Sohlman chose not to write to the two institutional winners, as opposed to the individual winners, of the Nobel Peace Prize: the Institute of International Law in 1904 and the Permanent International Peace Bureau in 1910.

Once the date for submissions had passed on 10 December 1911, Sohlman contacted Montelius to ask him to convene his selection committee, as the two men had previously agreed. They had, of course, seen each other frequently over the preceding decade in the context of their work together for the Nobel Foundation. From time to time, Montelius would discreetly update Sohlman on the latest speculations relating to Stonehenge, albeit with the appropriate caveats attached. A significant advance had occurred, however, with the investigations conducted by William Gowland, an English mining engineer and amateur archaeologist. On 31 December 1900, one of the largest stones still upright at Stonehenge fell unexpectedly during a fierce windstorm. As another sarsen was left leaning precariously, Gowland had been hired by the Antrobus family to oversee its straightening. The task required resetting the stone in concrete, and the requisite digging would provide an opportunity for Gowland to conduct what became a sophisticated archaeological excavation. As Montelius explained to Sohlman, Gowland's observations (published extensively in the journal *Archaeologia* in 1902) had convincingly established that Stonehenge was much older than originally believed.

As for Sohlman, he, in turn, had alerted Montelius each time he received one of the four above-mentioned submissions. There was also an odd communication that had arrived early in the course of the competition. It was a short letter accompanied by a hand-drawn illustration. Given the address supplied by the correspondent, Sohlman had felt obliged to arrange the letter's translation into Swedish. The original had been written in English as follows:

Dear Mr. Sohlman,

It has come to my attention that a competition is unfolding with respect to solving the mystery of Stonehenge. As I have given substantial attention to the stone circles, I wish to offer my solution for the mystery of WHEN Stonehenge was built. I have previously established – when leisure has allowed – the astronomical orientation of ancient Egyptian and Greek temples. I have now established that a similar astronomical interpretation applies equally well to Stonehenge. Further, by means of certain measurements and calculations, I am able to date the construction of Stonehenge.

The argument is straightforward. Stonehenge was a solar temple built to observe sunrise on the longest day of the year – commonly referred to as midsummer or the day on which the summer solstice occurs. The grounds for this conclusion can be drawn from the confluence of the following observations:

– It was important that in ancient times, as now, those farming the land should know the suitable time for undertaking their different agricultural operations. It was the priests who were knowledgeable in such matters, by erecting temples (observatories) built specifically to observe the solstices and equinoxes – dates which marked the passage of one season to the next.

– As it is the longest day of the year that is easiest to fix by astronomical observation, Stonehenge was built so that the light from the sun rising at the height of

midsummer perfectly penetrated its axis from one side to the other.

– To this very day, people who live in the vicinity of Amesbury go to observe and celebrate the summer solstice at Stonehenge. It can therefore be assumed that sun-worship and ceremonies of prayer and sacrifice were once even more connected to the object of Stonehenge. Consider, for example, the numerous traditions that associate the mistletoe of the Druids with worship at Stonehenge. As the Druids hold the mistletoe that grows on oaks most sacred, and as the leaves of the oak trees are in full size at the time of the summer solstice, such considerations as these also support Stonehenge having been built as a solar temple.

Given the above inarguable facts, we can now reasonably surmise that the priest-astronomers who constructed Stonehenge accurately aligned the principal outlook of its stones – i.e., the main axis – upon the point of the midsummer sunrise. The azimuth of this main axis is 49° 34' 18" east of true North, easily measured due to its close coincidence with a line drawn between Sidbury Hill, the site of an ancient hill fort eight miles to the northeast, and Grovely Castle, another ancient fortification six miles to the southwest.

The geographic rationale for the calculation of the azimuth will be better apparent in the following sketch:

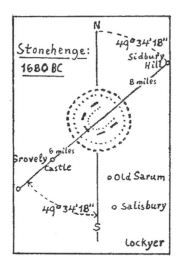

Most laypersons are aware that the midsummer sunrise marks the furthest point northward along the horizon at which the sun ever arises. It is less appreciated that over the past thousands of years, the point of midsummer sunrise is moving slowly eastwards. This movement is due to planetary perturbations, and the distance is measured as the Obliquity of the Ecliptic. As past values for the Obliquity have been calculated, it is possible to deduce the direction of the midsummer sunrise at any given location at any time in history. For the midsummer sunrise to have taken place at Stonehenge on an axis of 49° 34' 18" east of true North, the value of the Obliquity of the Ecliptic is 23° 54' 30.' Based upon published tables of the Obliquity, the date of the construction of Stonehenge is therefore 1680 BC.

As previous authorities have varied in their estimates with respect to the date of the original construction of Stonehenge by some thousands of years, I view the *accurate calculations contained herein as a significant advance.*

The author can be contacted should further details of the observations be required.

Sincerely,
Norman Lockyer

The arrival of Lockyer's letter had perplexed Sohlman. It was evident, of course, that the secrecy surrounding the Stonehenge Prize had been compromised. As Sohlman had neither contacted, nor even heard of Norman Lockyer, he immediately suspected Lady Antrobus as the source of the indiscretion. With some annoyance, Sohlman made a note to remind Lady Antrobus that only those who had won Nobel Prizes were eligible to compete for the Stonehenge Prize. Just as importantly, he would need to emphasize again that the very existence of the Stonehenge Prize was to be kept a secret.

As for the content of Lockyer's submission, Sohlman was unfamiliar with terms such as 'azimuth,' 'planetary perturbations' or 'the Obliquity of the Ecliptic.' Nor was it obvious to Sohlman how Sidbury Hill and Grovely Castle were connected with Stonehenge. Overall, Lockyer's confident but unusual assertions struck a discordant but increasingly familiar chord. As one of the directors of the Nobel Foundation, Sohlman was now aware that other such uninvited submissions were beginning to arrive in growing numbers at each of the official Nobel Prize selection committees. He had been informed that odd individuals were beginning to demand Nobel Prizes for the most bizarre and fanciful achievements.

At Sohlman's request, Montelius quickly reviewed Lockyer's solution. The notion that Lockyer had so easily determined 'the principal outlook' of Stonehenge seemed unlikely to Montelius, particularly as so many stones were now missing or significantly displaced from their original positions. In contrast to his crude diagram, Lockyer's measurements were suspiciously precise, as if to compensate for the imprecision of the underlying premise. The date of the submission – 21 June, the summer solstice – was also suspect and surely an attempt to mock the adjudicators. There were other objections, including what appeared to be a nonsensical reference to the 'full-size' oak trees. It was Lockyer's use of the term 'priest-astronomers,' however, that was most troublesome. There was simply no basis for concluding that ancient priests, if they indeed existed, were also highly sophisticated astronomers who were capable of designing and erecting an advanced solar temple. Despite Lockyer's confident assertions, the only reasonable appraisal was that Lockyer was simply a *knäppskalle* advocating a pseudoscience that wed stone circles with impressive, but vacuous, astronomical calculations. Montelius was decidedly unimpressed.

After learning of Montelius' poor opinion, Sohlman took a pen and wrote '*KNÄPPSKALLE*' at the top of Lockyer's first page. He then forwarded Lockyer's submission to the secretary of the Nobel Foundation. No further instructions were apparently needed.

CHAPTER 15

THE GRAND HÔTEL

On 10 February 1912, the meeting of the Royal Academy of Letters' Stonehenge Prize Committee began precisely at 3 p.m. in a small but elegant smoking room in Stockholm's Grand Hôtel. Although Sohlman and Montelius greeted each other warmly, Sohlman had not previously met either Axel Olofsson or Karl Sjöberg. Both men were established and respected members of the Royal Academy of Letters. Olofsson, elected in 1896, was a literary historian and a childhood friend of Montelius. Sjöberg, a member since 1902, was associated with Gothenburg University as a Professor in History and Political Science. He and Montelius were cousins by marriage.

Strangely, neither Olofsson nor Sjöberg had previously displayed the slightest interest in Stonehenge. Each was well known, however, for his friendly disposition and a willingness to co-operate with colleagues. Given Nobel's poorly defined instructions for determining the winner of the Stonehenge Prize, Montelius had concluded that the committee's final decision was likely to require a great deal of respectful discussion and consensus. In this light, the facility to co-operate would be paramount, and Montelius had chosen his two committee members accordingly.

There was also the matter of discretion. Montelius had represented the Stonehenge Prize to the Royal Academy of Letters as the idiosyncratic aspirations of an anonymous donor. Once the submissions of four well-known Nobel Prize winners were circulated to committee members, however, Montelius knew it would be impossible to continue to conceal the unusual nature of the competition. He had, therefore, elected to inform Olofsson and Sjöberg of the true genesis of the Stonehenge Prize at the time he had solicited their participation. Fortunately, as Montelius had anticipated, each man was flattered by his invitation and agreed not to divulge the secret behind the prize.

After brief introductions, Sohlman clarified that his own responsibilities would be peripheral to the activities of the committee. Aside from handling administrative matters as they arose, he would otherwise be inactive in the committee's deliberations and decision-making. Once the prizewinner had been determined, Sohlman would then resume his role as liaison to the four laureates whose submissions were now before the committee. Sohlman ended his remarks by reminding the committee that all matters pertaining to the Stonehenge Prize must, in all respects, remain strictly confidential.

As chair, Montelius then called the meeting to order. As the first item on his informal agenda, Montelius asked Sohlman to provide the committee with its instructions. Sohlman had anticipated this request. Based on Nobel's letter to Florence Antrobus, Sohlman succinctly presented the essence of Nobel's intentions as follows: to award a further prize to that Nobel Laureate 'who can solve the mystery of Stonehenge.' It was once again obvious to Montelius, and now to Olofsson and Sjöberg, that Nobel's words were frustratingly imprecise. Much of the three men's

Figure 23. Grand Hôtel, Stockholm.

subsequent discussion focused on interpreting the word 'mystery.' It was decided that any unanswered question concerning Stonehenge would be viewed as a legitimate 'mystery' for solution, and that such 'mysteries' would be conceptualized as falling into one of five categories:

- *Who* built Stonehenge?
- *When* was Stonehenge built?
- *How* was Stonehenge built?
- *Why* was Stonehenge built?
- *What* did Stonehenge represent?

There was one awkward moment. When Sjöberg suggested that *Where* Stonehenge was built might also be considered a 'mystery,' it was initially assumed he was either joking or introducing a nuanced consideration to the discussion. Regrettably, neither assumption would prove correct. Sjöberg knew virtually nothing about Stonehenge and would need to undertake considerable reading if he were to contribute meaningfully to the discussions.

The next item on the agenda was clerical in nature. Montelius asked Sohlman to distribute copies of each of the four submissions. Sohlman, organized as always, had translated each submission into Swedish and ensured that copies of the relevant illustrations were also included. Montelius then proposed that the adjudication process unfold as follows: each committee member would carefully review all of the submissions prior to their next meeting; the committee would then debate the plausibility, originality, significance and testability of each solution. The goal would be to generate a summative report, forwarded to Sohlman, with a clear recommendation as to which laureate deserved the Stonehenge Prize. With no objections raised, and with their business now concluded, Montelius moved that the committee adjourn for dinner. Sjöberg quickly seconded the motion.

Overall, Sohlman was pleased. He had anticipated that the day would be productive and had arranged for a special meal in the Grand Hôtel's elegant French-inspired dining room. The venue seemed particularly appropriate as the Grand Hôtel had been the site of the Nobel Banquet since the prizes were inaugurated in 1901.

With Sjöberg's faux pas now some distance behind them, the dinner began in a congenial manner. Once all were seated, Sohlman, as host, made a champagne toast to the king's health followed by the customary four cheers. Sohlman then proposed the men drink a more sombre toast in silence to the legacy of Alfred Nobel. Montelius responded with a toast to Queen Lovisa Ulrika, the Royal Academy of Letters' founding matriarch. An impressive meal then followed. Despite the considerable expense, Sohlman had requested that the chef recreate the elaborate feast served at the 1901 Nobel Banquet. This was periodically done on special occasions, usually for visiting royalty, and Sohlman had decided that the beginning of the committee's deliberations warranted such a celebration. After dining on significant *Hors d'œuvre*, the men were then served a series of elegant courses: *Suprême de barbue à la normande* (poached fillet of brill), followed by *Filet de bœuf à l'impériale* (fillet of beef imperial) and finally *Gelinottes rôties et salade* (roast grouse and salad). The dinner had begun with a vintage French Niersteiner (1897) and by the time the ice cream parfait and fruit tartelette were served, along with *Champagne Crème de Bouzy* (Doux et Extra Dry), the atmosphere at the table was buoyant.

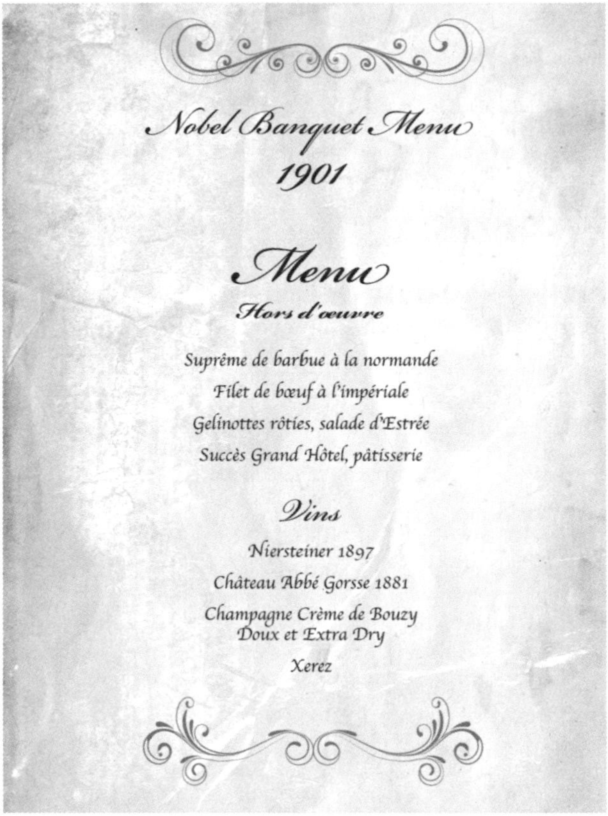

Nobel Banquet Menu
1901

Menu
Hors d'œuvre

Suprême de barbue à la normande
Filet de bœuf à l'impériale
Gelinottes rôties, salade d'Estrée
Succès Grand Hôtel, pâtisserie

Vins

Niersteiner 1897
Château Abbé Gorsse 1881
Champagne Crème de Bouzy
Doux et Extra Dry
Xerez

Figure 24. 1901 Nobel Banquet Menu.

Following dinner, and a rousing chorus of '*Dusie Prikaztjik*,' the gentlemen retired to an adjoining salon for coffee, sherry and cigars.[53] It was agreed that the next, and hopefully final, committee meeting would take place in approximately two months' time; at Montelius's request, the venue would again be the comfortable setting of the Grand Hôtel. Although Sohlman was invited to observe the new deliberations, he considered his attendance as unnecessary and politely declined.

The evening then ended with an unexpected but pleasant ceremony. Unknown to Montelius, Sohlman had already secretly commissioned the medalets he had agreed to provide to members of the Stonehenge Prize Committee. Duplicating the protocol he had observed at the Nobel Awards ceremonies, Sohlman solemnly presented the distinctive keepsake to each committee member as a preliminary gesture of thanks. Prompted by an enquiry from Sjöberg, Sohlman then informed the men that their more substantive monetary remunerations would be forwarded once the committee's final recommendation was received.

As the men left the hotel around midnight, Sohlman quietly asked Sjöberg if he would find it helpful to receive a small monograph on Stonehenge. A sheepish but appreciative Sjöberg indicated he would, indeed, be grateful for any such assistance that Sohlman might provide.

---

53. A reference to Freud seems obligatory. Freud's favourite cigar was the Don Pedros. Although the expression 'Sometimes a cigar is just a cigar' is associated with Freud, this attribution is likely apocryphal.

CHAPTER 16

TRIVIAL AND FLAWED

On 15 April 1912 the second committee meeting lasted a draining six hours. This time Sjöberg came well prepared, as did Montelius and Olofsson. In addition to each having reviewed the entire subject of Stonehenge, including the latest archaeological evidence, all three men had undertaken a careful analysis of each submission. As chair, Montelius had also made a number of specific requests during the intervening months. Sjöberg was asked to familiarize himself with the sea-craft of prehistoric England and the history of the Druids while Olofsson's assignment was to carefully read Darwin's observations of the earthworm. Montelius had left what he perceived to be the most difficult task to himself: tackling the law of radioactive decay.

In the end, Kipling's submission was dealt with quickly. The solutions proposed by Pavlov and Roosevelt proved more challenging to adjudicate as each raised questions of experimental validity and replication; in particular, Pavlov's research would require a year to duplicate while Roosevelt's daring proposition had yet to be tested. Curie's challenging theoretical work presented the committee with a different type of problem.

Stockholm
25 April 1912

Dear Mr. Sohlman,

It is my pleasure on behalf of the Stonehenge Prize Committee to submit our findings. As you are aware, we have been asked to assess the submissions from four esteemed individuals, all world-leading figures in their respective areas of expertise. The question at hand, however, is who among these individuals has most effectively contributed to solving one of the many mysteries associated with Stonehenge.

Before proceeding to the analysis of each proposed solution, it will be necessary to set forth the three key principles that guided our adjudication:

One: the wording of Nobel's intentions in his letter to Florence Antrobus served as the principal instructions of this committee.

Two: the 'mystery of Stonehenge' was understood to mean any unanswered question concerning Stonehenge.

Three: the value of each 'solution' was judged on the basis of the following considerations: the plausibility and originality of the proposed solution, the significance of the 'mystery' addressed, and whether the proposed solution lent itself to experimental verification.

With these principles in mind, the results of our deliberations are as follows:

Rudyard Kipling

Although reading the story of Puck was pleasant enough, Kipling's solution is simply a retelling of the notion that the Druids were responsible for building Stonehenge. There is convincing evidence otherwise. Gowland has now found that the implements used to dig the original stone-holes at Stonehenge were stone tools and picks made of deer antler. Given the absence of bronze or iron tools within the digging site, Gowland concludes – rightly in the committee's estimation – that Stonehenge MUST have been built prior to the transition from the Stone Age to the Bronze Age. This would mean roughly around 2000–1800 BC and, according to Graeco-Roman writers (Julius Caesar among them), at least a thousand years before Druidism flourished in Gaul and Britain. Kipling's 'solution' serves only to perpetuate a popular but unfounded myth.

Consensus: At best, an imaginative bedtime story for children.

Ivan Pavlov

The importance of accurately dating Stonehenge is acknowledged. The use of earthworms as a means to date an archaeological site is accepted as an interesting new instrument of measurement. The meticulous observations are deserving of admiration. But Pavlov's solution is found deficient on two accounts. As a first consideration, his approach is highly derivative. As Pavlov himself acknowledges, it was Charles Darwin who first entertained the role that earthworms might play at Stonehenge.

Secondly, Pavlov's in vitro experimental model (i.e., the flower pot) fails to represent the true in vivo conditions at Stonehenge, a landscape that includes the burrows of local rabbits and rodents and which for years has been aerated by tourists with hob-nailed boots. Such confounding factors would contribute to the rate at which stones settle into the ground, and likely more so than the action of worms. The extrapolations of Pavlov's in vitro results are therefore invalid and too flawed to warrant the one-year delay of experimental replication, which this committee considered and then rejected.

Consensus: Derivative, trivial and flawed.

Theodore Roosevelt

The importance of identifying the source of the bluestones and the means by which they were transported to Stonehenge is acknowledged. The use of an experimental methodology that allows results to be replicated is commendable. Roosevelt's supposition, however, is only as meaningful as the authenticity of his methods. He means to use only those techniques and means of transportation that would have been available to those who built Stonehenge. Yet the type of sea-craft proposed by Roosevelt would not have been used on the Irish Sea in prehistoric times. It was the skin-boat, NOT the dugout, that was then far more likely to be used for open-sea voyages of any distance, particularly over seas as rough as the Irish. Further, a raft of sufficient size to carry a bluestone would either be too wide or have a draught too deep to avoid grounding in the shallow waters of the rivers Avon and Wylye. There is a second and more serious flaw associated with Roosevelt's proposal: misconstruing myth for fact. Neither Mount Killaraus nor bluestones have yet been situated in Ireland. The magic of Merlin is an unfounded legend, not science. It follows that an attempt to transport 'any' type of stone from Ireland to Stonehenge – either by encouraging Roosevelt to test his hypothesis or by way of a committee-initiated expedition – is far too speculative and dangerous an exercise to consider.

Consensus: Untested, naive and foolhardy.

Marie Curie

As with Pavlov's submission, the importance of dating Stonehenge accurately is acknowledged. The committee, however, does not have the expertise to judge whether the sophisticated theoretical calculations and projections contained within the solution are intellectually sound. If valid, the methodology proposed would appear to have significant and far-reaching implications.

Consensus: Deferred.

Final Recommendation

The solutions proposed by Kipling, Roosevelt and Pavlov do not warrant further consideration. Though Curie's solution is intriguing, the committee lacks the competency to judge whether the role of radioactive decay in dating Stonehenge is a valid consideration. Appropriate expert opinion in the area of theoretical physics is required. The *committee therefore recommends that an authority such as Professor Svante Arrhenius now be consulted.*

Oscar Montelius
(on behalf of Axel Olofsson and Karl Sjöberg)

A disappointed Sohlman had hoped for closure. Nevertheless, he recognized the decisions and final recommendation as reasonable. Indeed, the committee was prudently utilizing an adjudication principle that was already in use for determining the Nobel Prizes: the appointment of an expert, when necessary, to assist in a prize-awarding committee's deliberations and decisions.

CHAPTER 17

ALBERT EINSTEIN

In almost every other circumstance, the Stonehenge Prize committe's recommendation of Svante Arrhenius as a consulting expert would have been an excellent choice. A winner of the Nobel Prize for Chemistry in 1903, Arrhenius was one of Sweden's most influential scientists. He was also intimately familiar with the principles of radioactivity. Not only had he been a member of the Nobel Committee for Physics since its inception, Arrhenius also functioned as an informal advisor to the Nobel Committee for Chemistry and, in that capacity, had recently conferred on the merits of Curie's investigations concerning the nature of radium. Despite the relevance of his expertise, however, Sohlman was reluctant to contact Arrhenius on two accounts. First, Sohlman was anxious to maintain the Stonehenge Prize as a distinct and private entity. Involving Arrhenius, a Swede enmeshed in the adjudication process of the Nobel prizewinners, would serve only to blur further the boundary between the Stonehenge Prize and the official Nobel Prizes.

The second reason for Sohlman's hesitation was more distasteful. After it was announced that Curie was to receive the 1911 Nobel Prize for Chemistry, excerpts of the private love letters between Curie and Paul Langevin were published in a Paris weekly. News of this correspondence quickly reached Sweden, and Arrhenius, ostensibly on behalf of the Royal Swedish Academy of Sciences, had prudishly written to Curie to suggest that she refuse the prize until her name was cleared.[54] Incensed, Curie had replied that she was unwilling to accept 'the idea in principle that the value of scientific work should be influenced by libel and slander.' Despite feeling unwell, Curie attended the Nobel ceremonies in Stockholm and responded graciously to the other scientists and dignitaries she met with one exception: an offended Curie refused to shake Arrhenius's outstretched hand of congratulation.

Montelius and his committee appeared to be unaware of these recent unpleasantries. Sohlman, however, had been apprised of Arrhenius's inappropriate intervention and was pleased that Curie had attended the Nobel ceremonies. Indeed, the incident had exacerbated Sohlman's existing concerns that the gender biases and moral double standards held by many on what were then exclusively male Nobel Committees were jeopardizing the selection of worthy female candidates, emancipated or otherwise.[55]

As soliciting Arrhenius's expert opinion of Curie's solution was now unthinkable, Sohlman considered the options available to him. In order to avoid potential entanglements with the existing Nobel Prize infrastructure, it seemed

---

54. Of interest, Arrhenius's first marriage to Sofia Rudbeck (a former pupil) had ended in divorce largely due to his opposition to Sofia's interest in pursuing an independent professional career. Once again, Freud's concept of 'displacement' (in this case, anger) looms large.

55. In an earlier iteration of his will, Nobel had explicitly specified that prizes were to be bestowed to the most deserving, whether 'a Swede or a foreigner, a man or a woman.' Although the last clause was omitted in Nobel's final will, it was well understood that those nominating and evaluating Nobel Prize candidates were to disregard gender (and nationality) in their considerations. Yet, as of 1912, only three women had won a Nobel Prize.

simplest to select an expert who lived beyond the borders of Sweden. With this criterion in mind, Sohlman reviewed the names of those theoretical physicists who had been recently nominated for a Nobel Prize in Physics. Among those proposed in 1910 was an Albert Einstein. Einstein had been born in Germany and was working in Switzerland at the time of his nomination. In 1905, as an unheralded patent clerk, he had published four seminal articles in the scientific journal *Annalen der Physik*. Now collectively known as the *Annus Mirabilis* ('Miracle Year') papers, Einstein had made fundamental observations on Brownian motion and the photoelectric effect, and had single-handedly initiated the relativistic era in physics. Yet few physicists, let alone the public, were able to understand the complex theoretical concepts and mathematical calculations that underlay his radical observations.

Through his connections with the Nobel Foundation, Sohlman was quickly able to elicit the more private opinions of Einstein from those within Sweden's scientific community (Arrhenius excluded) without revealing the purpose of his enquiries. The international community of physicists was then small and there were few secrets, professional or personal. Sohlman soon learned that Einstein was universally thought to be brilliant, albeit too theoretical for those with a strong experimental bias. He was also reported to be irreverent, a bohemian by nature, unhappily married with two small children, possessed (so the rumours went) with a wandering eye and penniless. From Sohlman's perspective, it was, of course, the perfect resumé.

Sohlman's offer to Einstein was mailed to Prague as Einstein had begun working the previous year at that city's

Figure 25. Albert Einstein.

Charles-Ferdinand University. The letter, originally written in German, reads in translation as follows:

Strictly confidential
23 May 1912
Stockholm, Sweden

Dear Professor Einstein,

As one of the appointed executors of Alfred Nobel's estate, I am writing to seek your assistance in an unusual matter. In addition to establishing annual prizes for achievements in the fields of science, literature and the promotion of peace, it was also Alfred Nobel's wish that a prize be awarded to the individual who solves the 'mystery' of Stonehenge.

A competition with respect to the latter has ensued, the details of which must remain private. I am able to convey, however, that a number of 'solutions' have been received and the adjudication process has begun.

To that end, you will find enclosed a short manuscript from Mme. Marie Curie, twice winner of the Nobel Prize and of whose work with radioactive elements you will no doubt be aware. Mme. Curie's 'solution' has been read with interest but the scientific validity of her arguments is beyond the comprehension of our adjudication committee. Your opinion as to the quality of the enclosed thesis would therefore be much appreciated, bearing in mind that the 'mystery of Stonehenge' is understood to mean any unanswered question concerning Stonehenge. Be assured that only an abbreviated response is required and can be sent to my attention at the address below. I ask that you also return Mme. Curie's manuscript.

As a small gesture of thanks and compensation for undertaking what we hope will be a brief but interesting exercise, please find enclosed a cheque for 1,000 Swedish kronor. If it is of interest, you may also keep the small guide to Stonehenge that is included within this envelope. Finally, please note that Mme. Curie will not be informed that I have sought your opinion in this matter. Further, your response will be kept in absolute confidence. For a variety of sensitive personal and legal reasons related to Alfred Nobel's legacy, I politely request that this correspondence, and all matters related to it, remain absolutely confidential.

Yours sincerely,
Ragnar Sohlman
Norrlandsgatan 6
Stockholm, Sweden

As it happened, Einstein was not only familiar with Curie's work but the two had recently met in Brussels at the end of October 1911. The occasion was the first of the Solvay Conferences, named after their sponsor Ernest Solvay, a wealthy Belgian industrialist. Curie and Einstein were two of the twenty-one scientists in attendance and Einstein had been impressed with Curie's intellect. It was literally days afterwards that Curie's affair with Paul Langevin became a public scandal. In contrast to Arrhenius's response, Einstein immediately wrote Curie a letter of support, encouraging Curie to 'simply stop reading that drivel. Leave it to the vipers it was fabricated for.'[56]

---

56. Einstein and Curie remained supportive colleagues until Curie's death in 1934. It was because of Curie's recommendation that Einstein was able to leave Prague to receive his first full professorship at the Swiss Federal Institute

Einstein's admiration for Curie did not preclude the objective and candid opinion Sohlman had requested. Within a day of its receipt, Einstein had read and critiqued Curie's submission. Her manuscript was returned to Sohlman along with a short note written in German, translated into English as follows:

Prague, 30 May 1912

Dear Mr. Sohlman,

Thank you for the generous cheque and the opportunity to study and comment on Mme. Curie's submission. In brief, Curie's stimulating ideas have made a great impression upon me. They are as yet, however, too speculative to be accepted. That the radioactive element has yet to be determined is, of course, problematic. There is also a second matter of concern – Curie's calculations are dependent upon the radioactive element in question achieving a steady–state condition once it is absorbed in living tissue, and before the organism dies. This would seem to imply a similar steady–state condition must also exist within the earth's atmosphere which in turn would imply the likelihood of cosmic radiation as the generating force – a courageous set of assumptions that cannot yet be substantiated.

Regardless of the decidedly theoretical nature of her 'solution' – or perhaps because of it! – I hold Mme. Curie,

of Technology in Zurich. And it was through Curie's encouragement that Einstein joined (only later to resign) the Commission on Intellectual Cooperation of the League of Nations. Although most of their interactions were related to their shared intellectual interests, there were personal moments as well. In August 1913, Einstein and Curie, along with family members, hiked together in Switzerland. Though Einstein was fond of Curie, he once wrote that she 'has the soul of a herring.'

both professionally and personally, in high regard and will not be surprised if her conjectures are one day confirmed. As you have requested, I pledge to keep the circumstances of our communication a private matter.

With best regards, yours truly,
A. Einstein

One additional remark. Might Stonehenge have been constructed at a time when gravitational forces were reduced? The giant stones could have been lifted as easily as soup dumplings.

On reading Einstein's postscript, Sohlman laughed. He had forgotten that he had also been told that Einstein had an unusual and well-developed sense of humour. Even Montelius would smile when Sohlman shared Einstein's reference to the soup dumplings.

CHAPTER 18

DEAR LADY ANTROBUS

On 10 June 1912, Sohlman, Lilljeqvist and Lindhagen congregated in Lindhagen's law office for a final meeting. Montelius, representing the Royal Academy of Letters, was also present. Einstein's impression of Curie's submission, succinct but conclusive, was accepted. It was now clear that none of the laureates' solutions had sufficiently met Nobel's criteria to be awarded the Stonehenge Prize. Further, there was little enthusiasm amongst the men to extend the competition.

Before closure could be achieved, however, there remained one outstanding and contentious issue: the fate of the original submissions. As Lindhagen refused to consider their destruction,[57] Lilljeqvist favoured returning each submission to its respective applicant, an uncertain strategy as it risked reaction and further discussion. It was Sohlman who seized upon the perfect repository – and solution. Each submission would be added to the neglected and unread *Knäppskalle* file. The secrecy of the Stonehenge Prize would be preserved.

The following day, Montelius informed the Royal Academy of Letters – to little interest – that the competition

---

57. From Lindhagen's cautious perspective, civil or criminal proceedings were always a consideration. Should such legal proceedings occur, the spoliation of any evidence would have serious consequences.

for the Stonehenge Prize had ended and that none of the solutions under consideration had been found worthy. Sohlman also undertook one last task. After first visiting the Enskilda Banken (Private Bank) in Stockholm, Sohlman mailed the following letter to Lady Antrobus by registered post:

Strictly confidential
Stockholm, Sweden
12 June 1912

Dear Lady Antrobus,

I am writing to you again in my capacity as one of the appointed executors of Mr. Alfred Nobel's estate. As you are aware, an unusual competition has taken place over the preceding years. Due to an interest that you and Mr. Nobel shared, sixty winners of the Nobel Prize have now been invited to solve the mystery of Stonehenge. Regrettably, of the few proposed solutions received, no response was found to be of sufficient merit to warrant receiving the 'Stonehenge Prize' and our efforts are now at an end.

Nevertheless, those involved in executing Mr. Nobel's estate – Rudolf Lilljeqvist, Carl Lindhagen and myself – still wish to honour Mr. Nobel's interest – and yours – in Stonehenge. We are aware that Stonehenge is in a rather perilous physical state and that the costs of upkeep are significant. To that end, please find enclosed a cheque for 60,000 Swedish kronor. It has occurred to us that you and your husband might use the amount in some way to help maintain and protect this unique monument. We hope that such efforts will help ensure the survival of Stonehenge and, by extension, preserve the opportunity for the secret behind its mysterious existence to one day be solved.

For a variety of sensitive personal and legal reasons related to Mr. Alfred Nobel's legacy, I again politely request that this correspondence, and all matters related to its contents, remain absolutely confidential.

Respectfully yours,
Ragnar Sohlman

P.S. Please also find enclosed a small medalet that we hope will serve as a cherished memory of your good friend.

Although Lady Antrobus was ambivalent about accepting the funds, her husband – the fourth Baronet of Antrobus – was pleased. Unlike his father, this Sir Edmund no longer saw the upkeep of Stonehenge as a private responsibility, particularly given the decline of the Antrobus family fortunes. Stones that were leaning could now be straightened, those that were fallen could be raised, and a permanent custodian could be hired. Later that year, a series of support posts were installed at Stonehenge and a new fence was erected, one that completely enclosed the stones and surrounding earthworks. Unlike the rugged and broken picket fence it replaced, this barrier, 1,700 yards in circumference, was made of the lightest steel wire and was virtually transparent. On peering through its interlocking wires, those who visited Stonehenge could still gaze quietly upon the giant and mysterious stones.

Figure 26. Stonehenge.

PART FIVE

EPILOGUE

EPILOGUE

O ne of the more interesting challenges facing those clarifying the provisions in Nobel's will was the stipulation that the prizes were intended for those individuals 'who, during the preceding year, shall have conferred the greatest benefit to mankind.' Although it was clearly Nobel's objective to recognize works or discoveries of *recent* consequence, it was obvious to those tasked with interpreting the imprecise wording in Nobel's will that the definitive value of any particular achievement – be it a discovery, invention, improvement, work of literature or peace initiative – was not always immediately apparent. Indeed it was likely to take considerable time before an unexpected advance could be verified and/or its full ramifications recognized. To allow for this potential delay, thereby permitting *older works* to still qualify for an award, Nobel's emphasis on recent achievements was addressed in the statutes of the Nobel Foundation as follows:

> *The provision in the will that the annual award of prizes shall be intended for works 'during the preceding year' should be understood in the sense that the awards shall be made for the most recent achievements in the fields of culture referred to in the will and for older works only if their significance has not become apparent until recently.*

It was a thoughtful and prudent interpretation. Since the inception of the Nobel Prizes, the time required for the *significance* of an *older* work to be recognized has, not infrequently, proven to be lengthy. One example of the immediate confusion and resistance that authentic breakthroughs can produce is the research of Dr. Barbara McClintock. In the late 1940s and early 1950s, McClintock's findings challenged the notion of the genome as a static set of hereditary instructions. McClintock stopped publishing her startling results in 1953 due to fears that she was alienating her more conservative colleagues. Thirty years later, she was awarded the 1983 Nobel Prize in Medicine 'for her discovery of mobile genetic elements.'

With the benefit of hindsight, the solutions presented in this text can also now be recognized as the significant achievements they were. Despite the immediate impressions of the Stonehenge Prize Committee, Pavlov, Kipling, Roosevelt and Curie each anticipated an important development in our current understanding of the nature and origins of Stonehenge. The incisiveness of Curie's foresight – her supposition that radioactive decay might one day be used as a technique to date Stonehenge – is perhaps the most obvious. In 1960, the American chemist Willard Libby was awarded the Nobel Prize in Chemistry, 'for his method to use carbon-14 for age determination in archaeology, geology, geophysics and other branches of science.' Nine years prior to receiving his Nobel Prize, Libby had used his new science of radiocarbon dating to analyze wood charcoal thought to be contemporary with the beginnings of Stonehenge and estimated the date of the monument to 1848 BCE plus/minus 275 years.[58]

Ivan Pavlov also provided a means of dating Stonehenge, in his case employing a method based upon the presumptive rate at which its large fallen stones settled into the ground. Pavlov's earthworm-driven approximations now seem hopelessly crude compared to the advanced dating techniques currently used in modern archaeological investigations. Because of his fastidious microscopy, however, Pavlov usefully drew attention – literally – to the presence of pollen grains within an earthworm's digestive tract. Although Pavlov left unanswered the role that pollen might play as an archaeological tool, the analysis of pollen found in soil taken from archaeological sites is today routine. The uniquely shaped outer shell of a minute pollen grain is distinctive for each plant species and, given the remarkable ability of pollen to survive for millennia, its presence can reveal the flora once associated with even the most ancient ruins. For Stonehenge, such modern-day analyses have meant that the botanical landscape of the earliest days of the Stonehenge site has now been reconstructed. Of interest, the overrepresentation of plants associated with medicinal properties has been a significant argument marshalled by those who now propose that Stonehenge's principal purpose was as a site of healing.

In contrast to Curie and Pavlov's works that addressed the mystery of *when* Stonehenge was built, Roosevelt

---

58. In order to extend Libby's findings, other investigators have since conducted radiocarbon dating analyzes of antler and bone remnants found at Stonehenge. One analysis by a (unsuccessful) PhD candidate had Stonehenge erected just 200 years ago. The report was retracted after it became apparent that the bones analyzed were those of the Derbyshire Redcap, a distinct breed of chicken extant only since the eighteenth century; it is now believed these bones were likely discarded scraps, the detritus of Victorian picnics once popular at Stonehenge.

focused on *how*. Although Montelius and his committee dismissed his notions as foolhardy, Roosevelt's proposed simulation was, in fact, an important methodological innovation within the field of experimental archaeology. Consider, for example, the *Kon-Tiki* expedition, Thor Heyerdahl's successful bid to sail by primitive raft across the Pacific in 1947. Roosevelt's error was simply to have been so beguiled by the myth of Merlin. Erroneously sourcing the bluestones to Ireland based on a literal reading of Geoffrey of Monmouth's account overshadowed what was an otherwise valid effort to address one of the central mysteries of Stonehenge: where the bluestones had come from and in what way they had arrived.

Despite his apparent credulity, Roosevelt *was* prescient in appreciating the role of water transport in the bluestones' journey. In 1923, Dr. H. H. Thomas, a petrographer for the British Geological Survey, established that all variations of the bluestones present at Stonehenge could be found congregated on the slopes of the Prescelly Mountains of northern Pembrokeshire in south-west Wales, *not* Ireland. As Roosevelt anticipated, their most probable route from Wales to Stonehenge, roughly 135 miles away, appears to have included a significant journey by raft along the coastal shores of South Wales. Fittingly, Neolithic-costumed volunteers aboard 'Stone Age' boats are now testing the likelihood of this proposition.

The localization of the bluestones to an area a significant distance to the west of Stonehenge also establishes Roosevelt as less credulous than initially supposed. Like Ireland, Wales is west of Stonehenge. Further, there is some evidence to suggest Irish peoples settled the area around the Prescelly Mountains. Geoffrey's reference to Mount Killaraus in Ireland may have arisen from a historical reality that was gradually distorted as its memory passed from generation to generation. Given the approximate agreement between the legend and fact, Roosevelt can now be viewed as among the first of a growing number of historians who believe, almost certainly correctly, that myths and legends are frequently based on real historical events.

Compared to Roosevelt's contribution, the contemporary value of Kipling's submission – an imaginative but misguided retelling of Stonehenge as a Druidic temple – is, at first, less clear. Despite the still popular belief that Druids are linked with Stonehenge, the Stonehenge Prize Committee was correct in emphasizing that sarsens and trilithons of Stonehenge stood long before the existence of Druidism, a Celtic pagan religion first mentioned by classical writers about 200 BCE.[59] Within his fictional account, however, Kipling did usefully anticipate the discovery of Stonehenge's formerly unnoticed carvings. In 1953, Professor R. J. C. Atkinson was the first to draw academic and public attention to the faded imprint of a short dagger on the inner face of one of the sarsen stones. Eerily, the shape of the dagger that Kipling had Puck carve in front of Dan and Una bears an uncanny resemblance to Atkinson's finding. Whether Kipling imagined the dagger or actually detected its faint, weathered presence at Stonehenge is uncertain. Regardless of which explanation for its

59. A caveat is in order about the Druids: many experts believe Stonehenge served a religious and ritual function for various prehistoric peoples. Although the Druids arrived too late to have built Stonehenge, it remains conceivable that the Druids *did* appropriate the existing stone circles for their religious ceremonies, human sacrifices and all.

Figure 27. Carvings at Stonehenge.
Photographer R. J. C. Atkinson.

genesis is correct, Kipling's incorporation of the image into his story creatively foretold the subsequent recognition of Stonehenge's previously hidden carvings.[60] Perhaps even more prophetic was the nature of Kipling's field trip. In visiting Stonehenge, Kipling arrived by car. The attendant fumes and overcrowding associated with the subsequent onslaught of like-minded motorists has jeopardized Stonehenge's very survival.

As for Einstein, it seems unwise to doubt even his most whimsical musings. Gravitational forces on Earth *can* vary, particularly with latitude and altitude. Could a more profound and transient variation of gravitational forces have occurred sometime in the past, to the extent that Neolithic men could effortlessly position massive sarsen stones? The notion may be less preposterous than it seems. In anticipation of erecting a variety of structures on the Moon, NASA's astronauts are now training with crude building materials and equipment on construction sites within reduced gravity environments. The assembled configurations have an unnerving likeness to Stonehenge.

Of all the submissions forwarded to Sohlman, however, it was Norman Lockyer's solution that merited far more serious respect than the prejudice it received. Dismissed as a *knäppskalle*, Lockyer went on to publish an expanded version of his theory in a book titled *Stonehenge and Other British Stone Monuments Astronomically Considered*. His ideas were again disparaged and rejected. In 1966, however, Gerald Hawkins, an English astronomer, published in book form (*Stonehenge Decoded*) what appeared to be a convincing array

---

60. Most of these are the subtle outlines of tiny daggers and early Bronze Age axe heads.

of computer-generated calculations that positioned Stonehenge as an observatory. Hawkins's conclusions also initially met with controversy. Now, however, there is considerable support for the astro-archaeological arguments that Lockyer first put forward and Hawkins supported. In particular, the precise geometrical placements of at least some of the stones at Stonehenge allow for meticulous observations of major solar and lunar events, not the least of which is celebration of the midwinter and midsummer solstice.

There have been other significant developments in our understanding of Stonehenge over the past century. Advances in radiocarbon dating analyses now suggest that Stonehenge was built in three main phases (some argue five, some add subdivisions): Stonehenge I – the initial earthworks in 2950 BCE; Stonehenge II – a bluestone double circle in 2400 BCE; and Stonehenge III – the staggered arrival of the sarsens and the rearrangement of the bluestones over the next seven hundred years. Experiments have tested how the stones were transported, shaped and erected. Excavations have provided new clues as to the identity of those prehistoric people who used and visited Stonehenge. The importance of examining the role Stonehenge played in a broader Neolithic landscape has become more clear. New evidence and/or theories as to why Stonehenge was built, or what purposes it once served, have been put forward or re-emphasized: Stonehenge as temple, as Neolithic computer used to predict eclipses and other celestial events, as primitive cathedral, as a place for healing, as soundscape, as lunar and solar observatory, as calendar and as a resting place for the dead. Yet despite this proliferation in knowledge, uncertainty persists and the fundamental secrets of Stonehenge endure.

Perhaps the Stonehenge Prize merits resurrection. Nobel and Lady Antrobus would undoubtedly wish so. And perhaps, for this new iteration, so-called *knäppskalles* should also be encouraged to 'solve' Stonehenge, not just Nobel Laureates. After all, why preclude the likes of Norman Lockyer – or other perceived *knäppskalles* – from competing for the Stonehenge Prize? True, not all of Lockyer's observations were correct. Roman invaders are now known to have built both Sidbury Hill and Grovely Castle long after Stonehenge was constructed. Yet Lockyer used both locations (neither of which, as a puzzling aside, can even be seen from Stonehenge) as sightlines for his calculations, something the original builders of Stonehenge would obviously have not been able to do. Still, there was genius in Lockyer's madness. Madness and genius. Given the razor-thin line that separates the two, might there be other unexpected and extraordinary insights waiting to be discovered in the *Knäppskalles* file?

There is, of course, one additional matter that also merits resurrection: the question as to why Freud never received the Nobel Prize. According to documents in the Nobel Archives, Freud's work was viewed as *too subjective* for traditional scientific evaluation. The requisite delay in recognizing the value of the submissions for the Stonehenge Prize now suggests a better explanation. Rather than being too subjective for traditional scientific evaluation, Freud's work was *too advanced* for traditional scientific evaluation, or at least for the scientific methods of his era. Emerging modern methodologies, however, are now beginning to align Freud's fundamental concepts with objective neurobiological findings. Amongst the convincing discoveries, unconscious memory systems have now been unequivocally localized to specific areas of the brain. Even more remarkable, neuroscientists are on the verge of identifying the actual structural changes in the brain that occur during the course of psychotherapy.

Like those who competed for the Stonehenge Prize, Freud anticipated and enriched our understanding of a mystery, but one far more profound than the mystery of Stonehenge. Freud was intent on solving the mystery of the mind, and who today would be mad enough to deny Freud the Nobel Prize he deserves? Freud was right to implicate unconscious mental processes as critical factors for driving out motives and behaviours. And, I suppose I was also right to have followed quietly in Freud's footsteps as I cared for my patients. As I reflect on my life's work, I find that realization deeply satisfying.

Figure 28. Sigmund Freud.

POSTSCRIPTS

POSTSCRIPTS

Florence Antrobus	1856–1923
Marie Curie	1867–1934
Albert Einstein	1879–1955
Sigmund Freud	1856–1939
Sofie Hess	1851–1919
Rudyard Kipling	1865–1936
Rudolf Lilljeqvist	1855–1930
Carl Lindhagen	1860–1946
Norman Lockyer	1836–1920
Oscar Montelius	1843–1921
Alfred Nobel	1833–1896
Ivan Pavlov	1849–1936
Theodore Roosevelt	1858–1919
Ragnar Sohlman	1870–1948
Bertha von Suttner	1843–1914

Florence Antrobus 1856–1923

Florence Antrobus remained committed to the preservation of Stonehenge throughout her life. With the death of her father-in-law in 1899, her husband, Edmund, inherited Stonehenge and succeeded to the title of Fourth Baronet Antrobus. As the newly designated Lady Antrobus, she played an active role in the life of her community, frequently hosting public events on the grounds of Amesbury Abbey. She would also occasionally submit articles and letters to women's magazines: one entry concerning the Dreyfus affair that was published in the weekly journal *The Gentlewoman* netted her a complimentary three-month subscription. Her crowning literary achievement, however, was a small self-published monograph, *A Sentimental and Practical Guide to Amesbury and Stonehenge.*

On 24 October 1914, Lady Antrobus lost her only child (Lieutenant Edmund Antrobus) in action at Ypres. Her husband died less than four months later. The Fifth Baronet Antrobus, Sir Cosmos Antrobus, immediately attempted to sell the entire Amesbury Abbey estate in various lots. In 1916, Cecil Chubb, a local resident, purchased Stonehenge and thirty surrounding acres for £6,600. Two years later Chubb donated Stonehenge to the British government.

Florence Antrobus died in 1923. Her funeral was held in Amesbury Abbey Church, following which her coffin was placed in the Antrobus family vault on the grounds of the churchyard, just a short distance from Stonehenge. In her will she bequeathed funds to establish Antrobus House, a public museum dedicated to her son Edmund's memory. It is now Amesbury's premier events venue and available for hire.

Marie Curie 1867–1934

After returning from Stockholm in 1911, Curie continued to dedicate her life to the study of radiation and its applications. During

World War I, she pioneered the use of mobile X-ray units, risking her safety travelling to the front lines throughout France in makeshift ambulances. Following the war, she was then active in the international peace movement and for twelve years played a leading role with the League of Nations' Commis-

sion on Intellectual Cooperation. Despite failing health, Curie made two celebrated visits to the United States in her later years to raise funds for the Institut du Radium, the Paris-based research facility established in her honour. In 1934, at the age of sixty-six, she died of radiation-induced leukemia, succumbing to the lethal side effects of her own discovery.

Curie's intimate association with the Nobel Prizes continued after her death. Her daughter Irène was jointly awarded the 1935 Nobel Prize in Chemistry with her husband Frédéric Joliot 'in recognition of their synthesis of new radioactive elements.' Thirty years later, Curie's other daughter, Eve, was with her husband, Henry Labouisse, when he accepted the Nobel Peace Prize as the Executive Director of the United Nations Children's Fund (UNICEF).

Marie Curie is still the only individual to have received two Nobel Prizes in two distinct scientific disciplines (physics and chemistry). Her papers and small personal effects are now on deposit in lead-lined containers at the Bibliothèque Nationale de France. Access to the archived material is subject to two preconditions: a signed waiver of liability and the obligatory donning of radiation-protective clothing.

Albert Einstein 1879–1955

Albert Einstein won the Nobel Prize in Physics in 1921 (awarded in 1922). Interestingly, the prize was awarded 'for his services to Theoretical Physics, and especially for his discovery of the law of the photoelectric effect.' Unique in the history of the Nobel Prizes, there was a caveat. Einstein's Nobel Prize was being presented 'without taking into account the value that will be accorded your relativity and gravitation theories after these are confirmed in the future.' Although the proviso preserved the possibility of Einstein winning a future Nobel Prize (he didn't), it also highlighted the uncertain significance then associated with what physicists now view as Einstein's far greater achievements, particularly his theories of special and general relativity (of $E = mc^2$ fame), published in 1905 and 1916 respectively.

Einstein had counted on winning a Nobel Prize. By 1914, he had separated from his first wife, Mileva Marić. As part of their divorce settlement, Einstein agreed that any future Nobel Prize money awarded to him would be put in trust for their two sons, Hans Albert and Eduard. The money proved badly needed. Eduard developed schizophrenia in early adulthood and thereafter required significant support, spending the last years of his life in the Burghölzli, a psychiatric hospital in Zurich.

Einstein died in Princeton, New Jersey, in 1955. His brain was illegally removed at autopsy and continues to be studied in the hope that an anatomical basis for his genius will eventually be uncovered.

Sigmund Freud 1856–1939

Once Nazi Germany annexed Austria in 1938, Freud was convinced by colleagues to flee Vienna for England. He would die in London on 23 September 1939 of inoperable oral cancer, a death hastened by large doses of morphine. Freud had endured the malignancy for more than sixteen years. Despite severe chronic pain and more than thirty surgical procedures, he had continued to smoke more than twenty cigars a day. Just prior to his death, Freud had presented his valuable collection of cigars to his brother as a last gift.

Freud's will contained few surprises. There was a small annuity for his sister-in-law, Minna, who lived with Freud and his wife. His daughter Anna, the only one of his six children to embrace psychoanalysis as a career, was to receive his collection of antiques and professional library. Otherwise, royalties associated with Freud's writings and his other assets were assigned in various proportions to his wife, Martha, and to his surviving children and grandchildren.

Though it contradicted the tenets of Orthodox Judaism, Freud arranged for his own cremation. His ashes were deposited in an ancient Grecian urn, one of the many classical pieces in his large collection of antiquities. When his widow, Martha, died in 1951, she too was cremated. As there was insufficient room in Freud's urn, only some of her ashes could be mingled with those of her late husband. Even in death, Freud's remarkable aura left little room for the presence of others, even those near and dear.

Sofie Hess 1851–1919

Little is known about Sofie Hess's life once her relationship with Nobel ended. She returned from Paris to live in Austria sometime in the late 1880s. Her daughter Gretl was born out of wedlock in July 1891. In 1893, she wrote to Nobel stating she intended to marry Gretl's father, Captain Kapy von Kapivar, in order 'to give her a name so that later on she doesn't have to be ashamed.' The Captain, after honourably marrying Sofie in 1895, retired from the cavalry to enter the champagne business, only to drown in the Danube.

Nobel, even when estranged from Sofie, continued to accede to Sofie's requests for money, albeit more and more impersonally. Finally, tired of Sofie's incessant petitions, Nobel provided Sofie with a stipend of 500 Hungarian florins a month. Nobel's last letter to Sofie was written on 7 March 1895. The short note congratulated Sofie upon her upcoming marriage, but even then his good wishes were tempered, as he urged Sofie 'to give up much of your conceit.' Following Nobel's death, Sofie resorted to blackmail. Claiming to be the equivalent of Nobel's wife, Sofie threatened to publish the correspondence between Nobel and herself unless she received a significant financial settlement. To resolve the matter, Sohlman arranged payment of 12,000 florins, a relatively modest sum especially given the refractory nature of Sofie's irresponsible spending habits. In return, Sofie agreed not to tarnish Nobel's reputation, a stipulation she apparently respected. As Nobel once wrote to Sofie, 'when all is said and done, you are a sensitive little creature.'

Rudyard Kipling 1865–1936

By the time Kipling received his Nobel Prize in Literature in 1907, his literary sheen was waning. According to serious critics, he had become too imperialist, too popular and too prolific. Kipling would also soon lose the playfulness that characterized such earlier writings as *The Jungle Book* or the *Just So Stories*. In 1915, Kipling's only son, John, an officer in the Irish Guards, went missing in action just days after his regiment had arrived in France to fight on the Western Front. John had failed in his initial attempt to enlist due to poor eyesight and Kipling had subsequently been instrumental in facilitating his son's commission with the Irish Guards. On learning John was wounded and missing, Kipling, plagued by a sense of culpability, was unable to accept the virtual certainty of his son's death. For years Kipling and his wife searched desperately for news, at one point arranging to have leaflets dropped over enemy lines seeking information on a Second Lieutenant John Kipling's whereabouts. Kipling's lingering guilt is palpable in this grief-stricken couplet from 'Epitaphs of the War, 1914–1918':

> If any question why we died,
> Tell them, because our fathers lied.

Following the war, Kipling travelled frequently throughout France, initially in his capacity as a member of the Imperial War Graves Commission and then for the pleasure of admiring the French countryside. He remained a motoring enthusiast throughout his life, preferring the Rolls Royce above all other vehicles. Kipling was about to embark on a winter motor tour in France in 1936 when he died suddenly of a perforated duodenal ulcer. His ashes lie buried in Poets' Corner at Westminster Abbey.

Rudolf Lilljeqvist 1855–1930

Rudolf Lilljeqvist was never quite certain why he was chosen to help implement Nobel's legacy. It was only after Nobel's death that he learned that he had been appointed an executor of Nobel's will. His surprising designation was conveyed in a cable he received from Ragnar Sohlman, a man then unknown to him but also appointed as Nobel's executor. To add to the confusion, Lilljeqvist's name was misspelled in the will. As Lilljeqvist responded in his cable to Sohlman, 'Do not understand your telegram. Am I mentioned in the will?' Despite Lilljeqvist's initial reservations, he brought an unsentimental and seasoned approach to his new responsibilities and his pragmatic opinions helpfully balanced Sohlman's more emotional and inexperienced inclinations.

Following the successful resolution of Nobel's will, Lilljeqvist's significant financial acumen was now devoted entirely to managing his own business interests. Although the electrochemical factory in Bengtsfors initially operated at a loss, it soon garnered substantial profits. By 1910, Lilljeqvist could afford to build Baldersnäs, a large mansion where he and his wife, Ellen Fredrika Wichman, would raise their five children. As one of his last business ventures, Lilljeqvist successfully expanded the number of generators powered by a hydro-electric power plant located close to his factory on nearby Lake Lelangens. In 1930, Lilljeqvist drowned in the hydroelectric dam's reservoir. His body was never recovered. Today, Baldersnäs is a luxury country hotel.

Carl Lindhagen 1860–1946

In addition to his prestigious legal career and his position for twenty-seven years as Chief Magistrate of Stockholm, Lindhagen was also a prominent Swedish politician, serving as a member of left-wing socialist parties in the Swedish parliament in the years 1897–1917 and 1919–1940. Lindhagen's political views were broadminded and radical for the times. His liberal causes included support for the female suffrage movement, the working poor, and the indigenous Sami people of Sweden and other Nordic countries. A pacifist, Lindhagen was also very involved in the international peace movement. He had a particular interest in the universal language of Esperanto, first promoted in 1887 by L. L. Zamenhof. Like Zamenhof, Lindhagen viewed Esperanto as an effective vehicle to overcome the potential barriers generated by disparate national languages. One of two million active speakers of Esperanto at the onset of the twentieth century, Lindhagen was given the honour of presenting the opening address at the World Congress of Esperanto in Danzig in 1927.

For his support of women's rights, social reform and Sweden's radical peace movement, Lindhagen was nominated for the Nobel Peace Prize an extraordinary eighteen years in a row, beginning in 1922. Though his prestigious nominators ranged from members of the Swedish, Norwegian, Lithuanian, Finnish and Estonian parliaments to professors of international law, Lindhagen still failed to win the coveted prize.

Norman Lockyer 1836–1920

Norman Lockyer was a creative thinker and prodigious worker throughout his life. Despite beginning his career as an amateur astronomer, Lockyer made seminal contributions in the field of solar physics and fathered the discipline of astro-archaeology. He also co-discovered helium and was the founding editor of the prestigious journal *Nature*. In retirement Lockyer established an observatory on a hill overlooking his wife's property near Sidmouth, a small town in southwest England. Now named the Norman Lockyer Observatory, it has recently celebrated its centenary and continues to serve as an important resource for amateur astronomers.

Of Lockyer's many accomplishments, least known today is his contribution to the game of golf. A member of the (now Royal) St. George's Golf Club, he was drawn to the sport because of the complex physics underlying a golf ball's trajectory. Frustrated by the inconsistencies in play he observed, Lockyer published a small hand-book in 1896 (with the assistance of a Mr. W. Rutherford) titled *The Rules of Golf*. Under the heading 'Etiquette of Golf,' Lockyer advocated the following: 'No player should play from the tee until the party in front have played their second strokes and are out of range.' The courtesy has survived and may represent Lockyer's most important legacy.

Oscar Montelius 1843–1921

In addition to his association with the Royal Swedish Academy of Letters, History and Antiquities, Montelius was also closely connected to Stockholm's Museum of Natural Antiquities, where he served as Museum Director from 1907 to 1913. His most significant research contributions revolved around his painstaking efforts to provide the relative and absolute dates of artefacts associated with the Bronze and Iron Ages of Northern Europe. One of the techniques Montelius promoted was the use of cross-dating, a means of determining the age of local artefacts by their association with objects whose dates could otherwise be derived from historical records, such as pottery that spread from Egypt.

Not everyone was enamoured with Montelius's meticulous approach to classifying artefacts. August Strindberg, the 'father' of contemporary Scandinavian literature, ridiculed what he viewed as Montelius's obsessive interest in minutiae. Strindberg mocked Montelius by equating him to a button collector whose days were spent classifying buttons according to size, composition and a range of other attributes. More serious concerns have been raised by contemporary archaeologists who now believe that Montelius's approach to cross-dating overemphasized the paradigm which holds that 'improvements' diffused from advanced civilizations to those less developed, a model that underestimates indigenous progress.

Montelius died in 1921. In keeping with his interests in the Nordic (or Northern) Bronze Age, he and his wife are buried in sitting positions in a *stendosar*, a type of stone grave used in Sweden during that period, the physical dimensions of which Montelius himself helped characterize.

Alfred Nobel 1833–1896

After Nobel died on 10 December 1896, a simple ceremony was held at Villa Nobel in San Remo, Italy. His embalmed body was then placed in a basic wooden coffin and taken to Stockholm by train. There, on the afternoon of 29 December 1896, a well-attended public funeral was held in the city's Great Church. Following the ceremony, Nobel's coffin was transported in a procession to Stockholm's Northern Cemetery where, in accordance with a provision in his will, his body was cremated. As Nobel had intended, this last act averted live burial with some certainty.

Despite Nobel's significant achievements as an inventor and industrialist, it was his grand philanthropic gesture that endures as his most lasting and important contribution. Today, a Nobel Prize is indisputably the world's most prestigious accolade. Yet, over the last century, the Nobel Prizes have also been associated with significant moments of controversy. Unfortunate errors of omission and commission in adjudication have occurred. Prizes have been declined, both voluntarily and on the insistence of authoritarian regimes. Changes to the statutes of the Nobel Foundation have also been made. A Nobel Prize can no longer be awarded to a nominated candidate who dies before the award is determined. It is now formalized that no more than three persons can share a Nobel Prize for any given year. In 1968, Sweden's central bank (Sveriges Riksbank) established a Prize in Economic Sciences in Memory of Alfred Nobel. The controversy associated with the introduction of the new prize prompted the Board of the Nobel Foundation to resolve that no additional prizes associated with Alfred Nobel's name will be permitted. The official status of the Stonehenge Prize remains to be clarified.

Ivan Pavlov 1849–1936

Although the 1904 Nobel Prize was his most celebrated achievement, Ivan Pavlov remained a productive scientist (and gardener) throughout his life. In his later years, his research interests shifted toward the induction of 'experimental neurosis.' After observing a dog's accidental near-drowning, Pavlov began to expose his dogs to life-threatening events. Pavlov equated the psychological after-effects in the traumatized dogs to the 'breakdowns' he observed in patients at a local asylum, anticipating by more than half a century the diagnostic syndrome now designated Posttraumatic Stress Disorder in psychiatric literature.

In 1920, after Pavlov threatened to emigrate from Russia due to impoverished work and living conditions, an embarrassed Bolshevik government was finally shamed into appropriately funding his research program. Despite this support, Pavlov continued to denounce a range of government policies, particularly Lenin's harsh repression of the Russian Orthodox Church. Toward the end of his life, Pavlov commissioned, and partially designed, a sculpture of a dog's likeness to commemorate the unselfish sacrifices made by 'Pavlov's dogs' in the name of scientific progress. The sculpture now stands in the garden of Pavlov's St. Petersburg laboratory, drawing more visitors than either Pavlov's own memorial or his preserved laboratory and study.

Theodore Roosevelt 1858–1919

After returning to the United States following his African safari and trip to Norway, Roosevelt was quickly drawn back into American politics. Disenchanted with the direction his Republican Party had taken in his absence, Roosevelt ran as the presidential candidate for the newly formed Progressive Party in the election of 1912. During the campaign, Roosevelt survived an assassination attempt, famously finishing a ninety-minute speech with a bullet lodged in his chest wall. Despite winning more votes than his Republican competitor, Roosevelt lost the election to William Taft, the Democratic candidate.

The following year, Roosevelt was persuaded to co-lead a scientific expedition in the Brazilian rainforests. He barely survived, losing more than fifty pounds as he fought bouts of malaria and the complications of a severely infected leg wound. On his return, his depleted physical condition so alarmed his physicians that they proscribed all travel. Despite this injunction, it required a further decree from President Wilson to prevent Roosevelt from resurrecting the Rough Riders and leading them into battle as a volunteer infantry division during World War I. After his youngest son, Quentin, died in action toward the end of the war, Roosevelt's warmongering finally subsided. He died in his sleep on 6 January 1919.

Memorialized as one of the four sculpted presidential faces on Mount Rushmore, Roosevelt is now best remembered for the stuffed toy animal he inspired: the teddy bear.

Ragnar Sohlman 1870–1948

Following his role in the successful realization of the Nobel Prizes, Sohlman remained involved in various Nobel enterprises. He first served as managing director of the weapons factory at Bofors, where he and his family would live in Nobel's Björkborn Manor for twenty-five years. Sohlman's other significant appointments were as the director general of the Swedish National Board of Trade and, for ten years, executive director of the Nobel Foundation.

A loyal employee and friend to Nobel, Sohlman initially suppressed the details of Nobel's relationship with Sofie Hess 'out of consideration for persons still alive.' Just prior to his death in 1948, however, Sohlman chronicled a number of revealing memories of Nobel, and included uncensored excerpts of Nobel and Sofie's intimate correspondence. Sohlman's explicit intent in doing so was to help shed light on Nobel's periods of depression in his middle and later years. The short memoir was published posthumously in 1950 under the title *Ett Testamente* (in English, *The Will*) and stands as the only intimate account of Nobel's private life. As Sohlman had feared, details of Nobel's involvement with Sofie provoked a great deal of salacious interest amongst the Swedish public.

Bertha von Suttner 1843–1914

Although Bertha von Suttner and Nobel carried on an amiable correspondence after her brief tenure as his secretary in 1876, the two saw each other again on only two occasions. The last of these meetings was in 1892. Bertha was by then a major figure in the international peace movement, largely due to the success of her novel *Die Waffen Nieder* (*Lay Down Your Arms*).

Published in 1889, the work was a well-researched indictment against war told through the eyes of its heroine, a fictional Austrian countess. Nobel was impressed with Bertha's articulate passion and, at her urging, he pledged to do 'something great' for the peace movement. He did; Nobel established what is now known as the Nobel Peace Prize in the final version of his will.

In 1905 Bertha became, fittingly, the first woman to win the Nobel Peace Prize (but not without wondering why she had been overlooked in the four previous years). In her Nobel Lecture, Bertha acknowledged Nobel as her friend and benefactor. Despite poor health, Bertha continued to lobby aggressively for peace. In 1912, she lectured throughout the United States on an exhausting six-month tour. Bertha von Suttner, Nobel Laureate, died on 21 June 1914, just one week prior to the assassination of Archduke Ferdinand of Austria and the beginning of a world war she had foreseen and dreaded. Delirious on her deathbed, her last words were '*Die Waffen nieder.*'

APPENDICES

A PSYCHOLOGICAL AUTOPSY:
A DIAGNOSTIC LISTING OF ALFRED NOBEL'S
DOMINANT PERSONALITY TRAITS,
DEFENCE MECHANISMS AND PRIMARY
MENTAL DISORDERS[61]

Ambivalence: *Simultaneous occurrence of contradictory desires, beliefs or emotions.* Nobel held distinctly mixed feelings for Sofie Hess throughout the course of their fifteen-year relationship; at times he would profess love, at other times irritation and disdain. Nobel's close but embattled association with Sofie ended only on news of Sofie's affair with Captain Kapy von Kapivar and the birth of the Captain's and Sofie's illegitimate child. Despite this betrayal, Sofie continued to receive an annual remittance from Nobel while he was still alive and was one of the eighteen beneficiaries listed in his will.

Delusional Disorder, Jealous Type: *The fixed and false belief that one's sexual partner is unfaithful.* Nobel's troubled relationship with Sofie Hess was complicated by intense jealousy. Nobel would routinely receive reports of Sofie's movements by engaging the concierge at

---

61. As just one of Freud's many accomplishments, he is credited with writing the first psychobiography. Freud's *Leonardo da Vinci and a Memory of His Childhood* (1909) is a detailed account of Leonardo's emotional life written from a psychoanalytic perspective. Nobel's emotional life can also be usefully constructed using key Freudian concepts that can now dovetail with the contemporary diagnostic criteria of mental disorders. The psychological/psychiatric definitions used in this Appendix have been adapted from the American Psychiatric Association's *DSM-5* (2013) and Salman Akhtar's *Comprehensive Dictionary of Psychoanalysis* (2009).

her apartment as a paid informant. He also employed additional spies to monitor her outings. Once, on receiving an unusually well-written telegram from the grammatically challenged Sofie, Nobel's suspicions reached delusional proportions. Convinced that Sofie could not have composed the cable without assistance, Nobel angrily accused Sofie of having an educated lover, or at least one capable of impeccable grammar and punctuation (see Footnote 16, p. 54).

Delusional Disorder, Jealous Type in Full Remission: *This modifier to the course of Delusional Disorder, Jealous Type, is applied when there is no longer the fixed and false belief that one's sexual partner is unfaithful.* Once Sofie began her affair with Captain Kapy von Kapivar, Nobel's beliefs about her infidelity were no longer false. In consequence, his diagnosis of Delusional Disorder, Jealous Type could be reasonably viewed as cured (see preceding two entries).[62]

Guilt: *An unpleasant emotion that derives from a real or imagined moral transgression.* Although Nobel's conscious experience of guilt fluctuated (see Repression, below), its pervasive unconscious presence can be inferred from a number of his obvious efforts at reparation. Most notably, Nobel's legacy included the Nobel Peace Prize. Although it was inspired by Bertha von Suttner's involvement in the peace movement, the Peace Prize was also a last-minute *mea culpa* for the weapons of death and destruction Nobel had introduced into the world.

Major Depressive Disorder, Recurrent: *Periods of depressed mood or loss of interest or pleasure associated with various cognitive and behavioural symptoms, such as decreased appetite, sleep, energy and concentration and the belief that life may no longer be worth living.* Nobel experienced significant bouts of depression throughout his life, particularly in middle age, and at one point had contemplated suicide. Nobel, even when crippled by depression, had – true to form – considered the

---

62. As Freud said: 'The paranoid is never entirely mistaken.'

commercial opportunities. As part of a disturbing fantasy, Nobel envisioned plans to establish a 'mercy clinic for suicides.' This would be an elegant establishment equivalent to a small luxury hotel with one consequential difference: staff would determine when to assist a guest's euphemistic 'departure' by administering a fatal injection.

Munchausen's Syndrome: *Otherwise known as Factitious Disorder Imposed on Self, this rare disorder is characterized by physical symptoms that are intentionally produced or feigned in order to assume the role of an ill individual.* In a letter written to Sofie Hess, Nobel stated that the stains of blood on one of its pages were due to one of his frequent nosebleeds. Strangely, the splash marks that are pathognomonic for authentic drops of fallen blood are absent. The most likely explanation is that Nobel himself deliberately placed the blood drops onto the paper with a scientific instrument, possibly with a pipette. This bizarre subterfuge was apparently a pathetic effort by Nobel to elicit Sofie's sympathy for his various physical ailments.

Nightmares: *Frightening dreams.* For the last six years of his life, Nobel was haunted by a recurrent nightmare of an ant repetitiously chanting in his left ear, 'It's against the law to pinch the biker, it's against the law to pinch the biker ...' Freud would have interpreted the ant as the symbolic equivalent of Nobel's diligence, and the reference to the law as an embodiment of Nobel's fears of scurrilous lawyers. The meaning of the 'biker' is less clear, and may either be an allusion to Nobel's financial involvement in a floundering bicycle-manufacturing company or, more likely, a lurid sexual fantasy that requires more exploration.

Nobel Prize Complex: *A set of character traits seen in some extremely gifted individuals that includes highly ambitious goals.* As delineated in Nobel's will, there is a subtle distinction in the criteria for winning a Nobel Prize in Physics versus Chemistry. Whereas the Nobel Prize for Physics was to be awarded on the basis of 'the most important discovery or invention,' the Nobel Prize for Chemistry was to be awarded on the basis of 'the most important chemical discovery or improvement.' Although the Italian chemist Sobrero 'discovered' nitroglycerine, it was Nobel's 'improvement' that led to its practical applications. Given the careful and nuanced wording of his criteria, Nobel was, in essence, positioning himself for a posthumous Nobel Prize in Chemistry (although, ironically, the statutes of the Nobel Foundation that were required to clarify the provisions in Nobel's will would preclude this possibility). Years later, the pathological need for recognition on a grand scale was recognized as a distinct nosological entity in the psychiatric literature. Deemed the 'Nobel Prize Complex' by the analyst Helen Tartakoff, the designation was used to describe those individuals – like Alfred Nobel – who had outstanding intellectual gifts and were also intensely driven to succeed (and be seen to succeed).

Oedipus Complex, Unresolved: *The Oedipus Complex describes the competition that occurs between a father and a son for the possession of the mother during the phallic stage of Freud's theory of psychosexual development (age three to six years). The Oedipus Complex is unresolved when the son fails to acquiesce to the more powerful father.* Alfred was five when his father, Immanuel, left his family in an attempt to reverse the family's fortunes. Having precociously 'won' his mother in his father's absence, Alfred's relationship with his father was thereafter tainted by an unstated but intense rivalry. The most unpleasant incident occurred when Immanuel accused Alfred of stealing his method for detonating nitroglycerine. Though Immanuel retracted his allegation, Alfred's hostility toward his father began to take on murderous undertones (see Patricide, below).

Alfred's Oedipal triumph also contributed to his distorted interactions with women. Deeply devoted to his mother throughout his life,[63] Alfred never attained the authentic intimacy of a mature and loving relationship. While he likely copulated with the much younger

---

63. A loyalty decried by Freud as a euphemism for erotic incestuous longing.

Sofie whom he frequently reviled, Alfred's true love objects were women like Bertha von Suttner and Florence Antrobus, cultivated but unavailable figures who epitomized the idealized asexual fantasy.

Paranoid Personality Disorder: *A pervasive pattern of distrust and suspiciousness.* Nobel was wary of others throughout his lifetime, particularly lawyers and business associates. At one point, he experienced a brief episode of frank paranoia, accusing the intensely loyal Sohlman of divulging a closely held business secret to a competitor. Though Sohlman was blameless, Nobel refused to apologize.

Patricide, Posthumous Type: *The killing of one's father.* Even after his father Immanuel's death, Alfred continued to harbour ill feelings toward him. As a last act of hostility, Immanuel was the basis for a poorly disguised character in *Nemesis*, a play Alfred wrote toward the end of his life.[64] Nobel had conceived of *Nemesis* as a tragedy in four acts loosely based on the life of Beatrice Cenci, an Italian noblewoman in the sixteenth century. At the play's end, Immanuel's doppelgänger is buried alive, the very fate the real Immanuel most feared while alive (as it was Alfred's, see Taphophobia, below). *Nemesis*, the play, fared just as poorly as the doppelgänger. Unable to find a publisher for *Nemesis*, Nobel proceeded with a private printing but he died just before the books were to be distributed for sale. His heirs were concerned the badly written play's existence would reflect poorly on Nobel's legacy. To protect Uncle Alfred, they purchased the entire print run and burned all but three copies.[65]

Psychotic Denial: *A pronounced break with objective reality characterized by the refusal to acknowledge some unacceptable aspect of external*

---

64. Alfred Nobel had longstanding literary aspirations that he had reluctantly set aside for his more lucrative business interests. His return to writing late in life was likely inspired by his interactions with Florence Antrobus.

65. Sparing the three copies appears to have been a mistake. In 2005, the play had a phoenix-like premiere in Stockholm: the reviews were dreadful.

reality or subjective experience. Nobel aggressively marketed dynamite and other explosives to governments and military forces around the world. Despite the obvious lethal consequences of his actions, Nobel continued to insist that dynamite was an agent for peace. According to his self-deluded appraisal, 'The day when two contending armies can destroy each other within seconds, all civilized nations will retreat from war and demobilize their armies.'

Remorse: *Moral anguish arising from prohibited acts.* Throughout Nobel's life, remorse was most notable by its absence.

Repression: *The unconscious expulsion of disturbing thoughts, wishes or experiences from conscious awareness.* Nobel's principal defence against anxiety was the unconscious act of repression (see entries on Guilt and Remorse, above).

Self-contempt: *Self-hatred.* As best illustrated by the following auto-biographical entry Nobel provided for his brother Robert's genealogical study of the Nobel family:

> 'Alfred N. – *pathetic, half alive, should have been choked to death by a humanitarian doctor when he first made his screeching entrance into the world.* Greatest accomplishments: *keeps his nails clean, and is never a burden to anyone.* Greatest faults: *lacks a family, a cheerful outlook and a strong stomach.* Greatest sin: *not worshipping Mammon.*[66] Significant events in his life: *none.*'

Sibling Rivalry: Competition between or among siblings for recognition or reward. The target of Alfred's most severe case of sibling rivalry was his younger brother Emil (see the following entry). Alfred also had lifelong combative relationships with each of his two older brothers, Ludvig and Robert. Most of the battles between siblings

66. A biblical term for material wealth.

were in the area of finance, with each brother vying for monetary supremacy, or at least control, over the family holdings.

Sibling Rivalry, Lethal Subtype: *Killing of one's brother (fratricide) or sister (sororicide).* Alfred's youngest brother, Emil, was blown to smithereens as a direct result of Alfred's reckless experiments.

Somatic Symptom Disorder (Hypochondriasis): *The preoccupation with the fear that one has a serious disease.* Nobel constantly complained of a diverse range of physical symptoms throughout his adult life. These included colds, stomach pains, double vision, rheumatism, motor tics, shortness of breath and insomnia. At times he believed he had congestion of the brain, which he treated by wrapping ice packs around his head and along his upper spine. In an effort to restore his health, Nobel frequented spas throughout Europe and would dutifully soak in strong mineral baths while he drank the local spring waters.

Taphophobia: *The fear of being buried alive.* As explicitly reflected in his will, Nobel had such an intense fear of being buried alive that he eschewed burial for cremation and was prepared to be bled to death as an additional precaution. Of interest, Nobel's taphophobia may have been on the basis of a familial predisposition, as his father had a similar fear throughout his life.

APPENDIX II

ACUTE RADIATION POISONING:
PSYCHOSOMATIC VARIANT

S tockholm, April 2013. Curie's submission was handwritten in French. After handling its pages for a number of days while rendering its translation into English, I began to notice tingling in my fingertips. It suddenly occurred to me one afternoon that, given the nature of Curie's research and her primitive laboratory conditions, her submission must have been contaminated with radioactive dust. It was a horrifying epiphany. That morning I had read that Curie's premature death was secondary to radiation-induced leukaemia: consequently, I, too, must now be exhibiting symptoms of radiation exposure. Alarmed, I immediately purchased nitrile gloves, rubber boots, a dust mask and a lead protective gown. I also bought a Geiger counter and dosimeter although I was unable to decipher the Swedish instructions well enough to operate either item.

The next day, I confronted (perhaps too excitedly) the director of the Nobel Archives and she agreed to forward Curie's submission to the Swedish Radiation Safety Authority in a lead-lined envelope. I was encouraged to be calm and to self-prescribe the necessary psychoactive substances to stay so. Three days later the Safety Authority confirmed that the document was 'hot,' although the contamination was at a level low enough to exclude health risks, with no need for protective measures when handling the document. Although vindicated, my relationship with the research staff cooled and I began to hear the word *knäppskalle* whispered as I left the Nobel Archives each evening.

There was one positive and gratifying development. At my request, the Safety Authority kindly dated the document using recently developed techniques that involved short-lived isotopes. The determination established with virtual certainty that the paper on which Curie's submission had been written had been manufactured sometime between 1910 and 1912.

AUTHOR'S NOTES AND ACKNOWLEDGEMENTS

In face of the incompleteness of my analytic results, I had no choice but to follow the example of those discoverers whose good fortune it is to bring to the light of day after their long burial the priceless though mutilated relics of antiquity. I have restored what is missing, taking the best models known to me from other analyses; but, like a conscientious archaeologist, I have not omitted to mention in each case where the authentic parts end and my constructions begin.

Sigmund Freud, from 'Fragment
of an Analysis of a Case of Hysteria'

This work of fiction owes a significant debt to the existing scholarship associated with the life of Alfred Nobel and his remarkable legacy. One of the key resources utilized was the biography of Alfred Nobel written by Ragnar Sohlman. In real life, Mr. Sohlman was the very determined principal executor of Alfred Nobel's will. Within this account, however, the role he plays with respect to the Stonehenge Prize is entirely imagined, as is the Stonehenge Prize itself. It follows that all other matters within this work that touch upon the Stonehenge Prize are invented.

For the early history of the Nobel Prizes, I relied heavily on the existing analyses of historical materials in various Nobel archives, particularly the work of Elisabeth Crawford and Dr. Carl-Magnus Stolt. Correspondence, books and documents related to Nobel and the Nobel Prizes were also consulted in the following libraries and repositories: in Stockholm, the Nobel Museum's Research Library; the Center for the History of Science under the auspices of the

Royal Swedish Academy of Sciences; the Nobel Library of the Swedish Academy; Riksarkivet (the Swedish National Archives); and Kungliga Biblioteket (the National Library of Sweden); and in Oslo, the Norwegian Nobel Institute library. Thank you to all those who so helpfully facilitated access to these resources: Kristian Fredén, Katarina Gustav Källstrand, Karl Grandin, Lars Rydquist, Thomas Lundgren, Bjørn H. Vangen and Inger Brøgger Bull. The opportunity to spend significant time in the Nobel Museum's Research Library was particularly appreciated (thank you, Kristian and Katarina).

For Stonehenge, the principal works utilized were *Stonehenge* by R. J. C. Atkinson, *Stonehenge Complete* by Christopher Chippindale and *Stonehenge* by Rosemary Hill. Many more articles and books contributed to its representation and to the portrayal of the various Stonehenge 'solutions,' including the prose of John Fowles; the images of Henry Moore; Charles Darwin's observations on the formation of vegetable mould; Norman Lockyer's astronomical considerations; Willard Libby's Nobel Lecture; and the charming supposition of Kilgore Trout (Kurt Vonnegut's alter ego) that Stonehenge was constructed in a time of very low gravity. Lady Antrobus was (truly!) the author of *A Sentimental and Practical Guide to Amesbury and Stonehenge*, first published in 1900. Lady Antrobus was a fitting docent – the Antrobus family owned Stonehenge for much of the nineteenth century. 'Poetical and picturesque' phrases from her 'little book' have been integrated into the Florence Antrobus–Nobel correspondence.

Freud's cameo appearances throughout the novel are often, but not always, grounded in truth. Although Freud's intellect hardly needs such buttressing, he is credited with a number of quotations and observations that were, in fact, made by others. It was Kahlil Gibran, for example, who said, 'the optimist sees the rose and not its thorns'; while it was Dr. Nathan Roth who recognized that there was no better document than the will to reveal the character of its writer. There are other significant liberties taken throughout the novel. Dates of real events have been changed (such as the sale of Tattershall Castle); life events of historical figures have been embellished, distorted or invented altogether; genuine quotations have been altered; the content of primary and secondary sources has been misrepresented; and, in the interest of verisimilitude and readability, Kipling's submission 'When Stonehenge was New' is, at times, a virtual pastiche of Kipling's own prose extracted from *Puck of Pook's Hill* and various other writings; in similar fashion, Kipling's invented letter to his son John draws heavily on the playful letters Kipling wrote to his children.

Thank you to the many scholars whose works are acknowledged by their presence in the bibliography.

Thank you to the following individuals and/or settings who kindly granted permission to reproduce the photographs within this work and/or assisted with their acquisition: Anne-Charlotte and Jonas Lilljeqvist; Jonna Petterson and Siavash Pournouri, The Nobel Foundation; Alexandra Franzén and David Larsson, Swedish National Heritage Board; Katinka Ahlbom and Torbjörn Altrén, National Library of Sweden; Ulf Larsson, Nobel Museum; Rita Aspen, Freud Museum London; Jim Fuller and The Lady Antrobus House Charitable Trust; Nils Johansson, Grand Hôtel Stockholm; Special Collections, University of Exeter; and Cambridge University Press.

Thank you to the following individuals who kindly aided the progression of this work: the remarkably generous Joseph Berg, Caroline Coutts, Paul Croteau, Guy Gavriel Kay, Anne Lennox and Jane Sayers; the staff at the library of the College of Physicians and Surgeons of British Columbia; David Boulton, Daniel Corrin, John Court, Celina Dunn, Rachel Faulkner, Peter Goodhugh, Sherri Hayden, Jason Hegardt, Paul Horrobin, Gustav Källstrand, Evan Munday, Patrik Nordstrom, Mike Richards, Kim Sparks, Anne Stone and John Walker; fellow SFU Writer's Studio alumni Berenice Freedome, Helen Heffernan, Anne Hopkinson, Antonia Levi, Caroline Purchase and ElJean Dodge Wilson; my supportive literary agents Carolyn Swayze and Kris Rothstein at the Carolyn Swayze Literary Agency; my siblings Karen, Ellen and Amy; and Sally, Franny, April and Elizabeth Karlinsky.

Special thanks to Catherine MacDonald, whose original drawings are an essential extension of this book's temperament and to my editors Scott Pack at HarperCollins U.K. imprint The Friday Project and Alana Wilcox at Coach House Books.

Sadly, Freud never did receive the Nobel Prize in Medicine or for Literature. Less sadly, Stonehenge's eerie mysterious presence endures. As for the 'Crackpot' file, I first came across a passing reference to its existence in an article written by Elisabeth Crawford. Each of the Nobel Prize–awarding bodies continues to receive an inordinate number of self-nominations. This interesting phenomenon merits investigation of a much more serious nature than that found in the present fiction.

SOURCES FOR QUOTATIONS

Epigraph

'They look upon me as pretty much of a monomaniac …': Masson, *The Complete Letters of Sigmund Freud to Wilhelm Fliess, 1887–1894*, 74.

Introduction

'Proposals received for the award of a prize …': 'The Nobel Foundation – Statutes.' www.nobelprize.org/nobel_organizations/nobelfoundation/statutes.html

'A prize-awarding body may, however …': 'The Nobel Foundation – Statutes.' www.nobelprize.org/nobel_organizations/nobelfoundation/statutes.html

'one of the fallen Druidical stones at Stonehenge': Darwin, *The Formation of Vegetable Mould, Through the Action of Worms, with Observations on Their Habits*, 156.

'From error to error, one discovers the entire truth': Brill, *John Huston's Filmmaking*, 189.

Chapter 1 Alfred Nobel

'Finally, it is my express wish …': 'Full Text of Alfred Nobel's Will,' http://www.nobelprize.org/alfred_nobel/will/will-full.html

'At the age of 54, when one is completely alone in the world …': Sohlman, *The Legacy of Alfred Nobel*, 46.

'the most powerful …': Freud, *The Ego and the Id*, 49.

'Isn't it the irony of fate …': Sohlman, *The Legacy of Alfred Nobel*, 39.

Chapter 2 Lilljeqvist and Sohlman

'As Executors of my testamentary dispositions, …': 'Full Text of Alfred Nobel's Will,' http://www.nobelprize.org/alfred_nobel/will/will-full.html

'red-taped parasites,' Schück et al., *Nobel – The Man and His Prizes*, 21.

'Alas, my health is so poor again…': Sohlman, *The Legacy of Alfred Nobel*, 39.

Chapter 3 Nobel's Last Will and Testament

'The whole of my remaining realizable estate …': 'Full Text of Alfred
Nobel's Will,' www.nobelprize.org/alfred_nobel/will/will-full.html

'Your Majesty – I will not expose my family …': Sohlman, *The Legacy of
Alfred Nobel*, 133.

'The long struggle …': Ibid., 135.

Chapter 4 'Frau Sofie' and Countess Bertha Kinsky

'had no further claims against the estate …': Sohlman, *The Legacy of
Alfred Nobel*, 78.

'It doesn't require much wit …': Ibid., 61.

'old philosopher,' Ibid., 63.

'It is clear to everyone who knows the circumstances …': Ibid., 76.

'A wealthy and highly educated old gentleman …': Ibid., 54.

'Alfred Nobel made a very good impression on me …': Ibid., 55.

'everything possible to amuse and entertain him': Ibid., 57.

Chapter 5 Stonehenge for Sale

'dark, mysterious forms'; 'the magic of Stonehenge': Antrobus, *A Sentimental and Practical Guide to Amesbury and Stonehenge*, 20.

'The Druid's groves are gone …': Byron, *The Poetical Works of Lord Byron*,
656.

'feebly in words': Antrobus, *A Sentimental and Practical Guide to Amesbury
and Stonehenge*, 19.

Chapter 6 Florence Antrobus

'the wild, tempestuous autumnal gales that usually sweep across the
Plain in October': Antrobus, *A Sentimental and Practical Guide to
Amesbury and Stonehenge*, 20.

'pleasure in reading': Ibid., 42.

'poetical and picturesque': Ibid., 19.

Chapter 7 The Secret Codicil

'I should like to will …': Larson, *Alfred Nobel: Networks of Innovation*, 202.

'Always keep in mind …': Sohlman, *The Legacy of Alfred Nobel*, 81.

Chapter 9 *A Sentimental and Practical Guide to Stonehenge*

'priceless Stonehenge': Antrobus, *A Sentimental and Practical Guide to
Amesbury and Stonehenge*, 19.

Chapter 10 Great Stones Undermined by Worms

'in recognition of his work …': 'The Nobel Prize in Physiology or Medicine 1904,' www.nobelprize.org/nobel_prizes/medicine/laureates/1904/

'Some ten years ago the great man …': 'Ivan Pavlov – Nobel Lecture: Physiology of Digestion': www.nobelprize.org/nobel_prizes/medicine/laureates/1904/pavlov-lecture.html

'At Stonehenge, some of the outer Druidical stones are now prostrate …,' Darwin, *The Formation of Vegetable Mould, Through the Action of Worms, with Observations on Their Habits*, 154.

Chapter 11 When Stonehenge Was New

'We have to go abroad next week for a few days': Kipling, *The Letters of Rudyard Kipling Volume 3: 1900–1910*, 282.

'in consideration of the power of observation …': 'Rudyard Kipling – Biography,' www.nobelprize.org/nobel_prizes/literature/laureates/1907/kipling-facts.html

'At this news I looked properly grave and sad …': Kipling, *The Letters of Rudyard Kipling Volume 3: 1900–1910*, 284.

'one of those motor-car things': Kipling, *Something of Myself and Other Autobiographical Writings*, 103.

Chapter 12 Seaborne Stones

'It shall be incumbent on a prizewinner …': 'The Nobel Foundation – Statutes,' www.nobelprize.org/nobel_organizations/nobelfoundation/statutes.html

Chapter 13 The Curve of Knowns

'in recognition of the extraordinary services …': 'The Nobel Prize in Physics 1903,' www.nobelprize.org/nobel_prizes/physics/laureates/1903/

'It can even be thought that radium …': 'Pierre Curie – Nobel Lecture: Radioactive Substances, Especially Radium,' www.nobelprize.org/nobel_prizes/physics/laureates/1903/pierre-curie-lecture.pdf

'in recognition of her services to the advancement of chemistry …': 'Marie Curie – Facts,' www.nobelprize.org/nobel_prizes/chemistry/laureates/1911/marie-curie-facts.html

Chapter 15 The Grand Hôtel
'Sometimes a cigar is just a cigar': Attributed to Sigmund Freud. See
   Wheelis, 'The Place of Action in Personality Change,' 1950.

Chapter 17 Albert Einstein
'the idea in principle that …': Quinn, *Marie Curie: A Life*, 328.
'a Swede or a foreigner, a man or a woman': 'Heroines of Peace – The
   Nine Nobel Women,' www.nobelprize.org/nobel_prizes/themes/
   peace/heroines/
'simply stop reading that drivel': Quinn, *Marie Curie: A Life,* 310.
'has the soul of a herring': Ibid., 348.

Epilogue
'who, during the preceding year …': 'The Nobel Foundation – Statutes,'
   www.nobelprize.org/nobel_organizations/nobelfoundation/statutes.
   html
'The provision in the will that the annual award of prizes …': 'The Nobel
   Foundation – Statutes,' www.nobelprize.org/nobel_organizations/
   nobelfoundation/statutes.html
'for her discovery of mobile genetic elements': 'Barbara McClintock –
   Facts,' www.nobelprize.org/nobel_prizes/medicine/laureates/1983/
   mcclintock-facts.html
'for his method to use carbon-14 for age determination in archaeology,
   geology, geophysics, and other branches of science': 'Willard F. Libby
   – Facts,' www.nobelprize.org/nobel_prizes/chemistry/laureates/1960/
   libby-facts.html

Postscripts
Marie Curie: 'in recognition of their synthesis of …': 'Irène Joliot-Curie
   – Biographical,' www.nobelprize.org/nobel_prizes/chemistry/laure-
   ates/1935/joliot-curie-bio.html
Albert Einstein: 'for his services to Theoretical Physics …': 'The Nobel
   Prize in Physics 1921,' www.nobelprize.org/nobel_prizes/physics/
   laureates/1921/; 'without taking into account the value …': Isaacson,
   Einstein: His Life and Universe, 314.
Sofie Hess: 'to give her a name so that later on she doesn't have to be
   ashamed': Fant, *Alfred Nobel: A Biography*, 279; 'to give up much of

your conceit': Sohlman, *The Legacy of Alfred Nobel*, 76'; 'when all is
said and done, you are a sensitive little creature': Ibid.

Rudyard Kipling: 'If any question why we died, Tell them, because our
fathers lied': Kipling, *Rudyard Kipling's verse: inclusive edition, 1885–1918*, 443.

Rudolf Lilljeqvist: 'Do not understand your telegram. Am I mentioned
in the will?' Sohlman, *The Legacy of Alfred Nobel*, 80.

Norman Lockyer: 'No player should play from the tee until the party in
front …': Lockyer and Rutherford, *The Rules of Golf*, 47.

Ragnar Sohlman: 'out of consideration for persons still alive': Sohlman,
The Legacy of Alfred Nobel, 52.

Appendix I

'The paranoid is never entirely mistaken': Rubenfeld, *The Interpretation
of Murder*, 62.

'mercy clinic for suicides'; 'departure': Hellberg and Jansson, *Alfred Nobel*,
120.

'It's against the law to pinch the biker, it's against the law to pinch the
biker …': Larsson, *Alfred Nobel: Networks of Innovation*, 7.

'the most important discovery or invention'; 'the most important chemical
discovery or improvement': 'Full Text of Alfred Nobel's Will,'
www.nobelprize.org/alfred_nobel/will/will-full.html

'The day when two contending armies can destroy each other within
seconds, all civilized nations will retreat from war and demobilize
their armies …': Hellberg and Jansson, *Alfred Nobel*, 95.

'Alfred N. – pathetic, half alive, should have been choked to death …':
Larsson, *Alfred Nobel: Networks of Innovation*, 10.

Author's Notes and Acknowledgments

'In the face of the incompleteness of my analytic results …': Freud,
'Fragment of an Analysis of a Case of Hysteria,' in *The Complete
Works of Sigmund Freud*, 12.

BIBLIOGRAPHY

Abramovitch, Henry. 'Bellow, The Therapy King,' *Jung Journal* 3 (2009, 57–67).

Abrams, Irwin. 'Bertha von Suttner and the Nobel Peace Prize,' *Journal of Central European Affairs* 22 (1962, 286–307).

———. *The Nobel Peace Prize and the Laureates: An Illustrated Biographical History 1901–2001* (Nantucket, Science History Publications, 2001).

Akhtar, Salman. *Comprehensive Dictionary of Psychoanalysis* (London, Karnac Books, 2009).

Albrecht. 'Das Großsteindenkmal Avebury in Südengland,' *Das Weltall* 14 (1914, 228–).

American Psychiatric Association. *Diagnostic and Statistical Manual of Mental Disorders: DSM-5* (Washington, DC, American Psychiatric Association, 2013).

Amis, Kingsley. *Rudyard Kipling and His World* (London, Thames and Hudson, 1975).

Antrobus, Lady Florence Caroline Mathilde. *A Sentimental and Practical Guide to Amesbury and Stonehenge* (Amesbury, Wilts., Estate Office, 1900).

Arnold, J. R. and W. F. Libby. 'Age Determinations by Radiocarbon Content: Checks with Samples of Known Age,' *Science* 110 (1949, 678–80).

Atkinson, R. J. C. *Stonehenge* (New York, The Macmillan Company, 1956).

Atkinson, R. J. C., S. Piggott and J. F. S. Stone. 'The excavation of two additional holes at Stonehenge, 1950, and the evidence for the date of the Monument,' *Antiquaries Journal* 32 (1952, 14–20).

Beck, Anna (editor). *The Collected Papers of Albert Einstein: Volume 5. The Swiss Years: Correspondence, 1902–1914* (Princeton, Princeton University Press, 1995).

Bodin, Helene and Stefan Torstensson. *The Nobel Banquets: Modern Recipes from Classic Menus* (Stockholm, Mixoft Publishing AB, 1998).

Boyko, C. P. *Psychology and Other Stories* (Windsor, Biblioasis, 2012).

Brill, Lesley. *John Huston's Filmmaking* (Cambridge, Cambridge University Press, 1997).

Byron, George G. B. *The Poetical Works of Lord Byron* (London, Frederick Warne and Co., 1912).

Chippindale, Christopher. *Stonehenge Complete* (London, Thames and Hudson, 2004).

Crawford, Elisabeth. *The Beginnings of the Nobel Institution: The Science Prizes, 1901–1915* (Cambridge, Cambridge University Press, 1987).

———. 'The Secrecy of Nobel Prize Selections in the Sciences and its Effect on Documentation and Research,' *Proceedings of the American Philosophical Society* 134 (1990, 408–19).

———. *The Nobel Population 1901–1950. A Census of the Nominators for the Prizes in Physics and Chemistry* (Tokyo, Universal Academy Press, Inc., 2002).

——— (editor). *Historical Studies in the Nobel Archives: The Prizes in Science and Medicine* (Tokyo, Universal Academy Press, Inc., 2002).

Crawford, Elisabeth, J. L. Heilbron and Rebecca Ullrich, *The Nobel Population 1901–1937: A Census of the Nominators and Nominees for the Prizes in Physics and Chemistry* (Berkeley and Uppsala, Office for History of Science and Technology, University of California, Berkeley and Office for History of Science, Uppsala University, 1987).

Cuny, Hilaire. *Ivan Pavlov: The Man and his Theories*, translation by Patrick Evans (London, Souvenir Press Ltd, 1964).

Darvill, Timothy and Geoffrey Wainwright. 'Stonehenge Excavations 2008,' *The Antiquaries Journal* 89 (2009, 1–19).

Darwin, Charles. *On the Origin of Species by Means of Natural Selection: Or, the Preservation of Favoured Races in the Struggle for Life* (London, J. Murray, 1859. 1st Russian ed. Rachinskii SA, translator, St. Petersburg, A. I. Glazunov, 1864).

———. *The Formation of Vegetable Mould, Through the Action of Worms, with Observations on Their Habits* (London, J. Murray, 1881).

Dossey, Larry. 'The Undead: Botched Burials, Safety Coffins, and the Fear of the Grave,' *Explore* 3 (2007, 347–54).

El-Hai, Jack. *The Lobotomist. A Maverick Medical Genius and His Tragic Quest to Rid the World of Mental Illness* (Hoboken, John Wiley and Sons, 2005).

Elzinga, Aant. *Einstein's Nobel Prize: A Glimpse Behind Closed Doors, the Archival Evidence* (Sagamore Beach, MA, Science History Publications, 2006).

Fant, Kenne. *Alfred Nobel: A Biography*, translated by Marianne Ruuth (New York, Arcade Publishing, 1991).

Feldman, Burton. *The Nobel Prizes: A History of Genius, Controversy, and Prestige* (New York, Arcade Publishing, 2000).

Fletcher, C. R. L., and Rudyard Kipling. *A History of England* (Oxford, Clarendon Press, 1911).

Flinders-Petrie, W. M. *Stonehenge: Plans, Description and Theories* (London, Edward Stanford, 1880).

Fowles, John and Barry Brukoff. *The Enigma of Stonehenge* (London, Jonathan Cape, 1980).

Freud, Sigmund. 'Über Coca. Centralblatt für die ges,' *Therapie* 2 (1885, 289–314).

————. *Jokes and Their Relation to the Unconscious*, translated by J. Strachey (New York, W. W. Norton. Original work published 1905).

————. *The Complete Letters of Sigmund Freud to Wilhelm Fliess, 1887–1904*, edited and translated by Jeffrey Moussaieff Masson (Cambridge, Harvard University Press, 1985).

————. *Leonardo da Vinci and a Memory of His Childhood*, edited by James Strachey, translated by Alan Tyson, with a biographical introduction by Peter Gay (New York, Norton, 1989. Reprint edition).

————. 'The Ego and the Id,' in *The Standard Edition of the Complete Psychological Works of Sigmund Freud*, vol. XIX, (1923–1925), edited and translated by J. Strachey and A. Freud (London: The Hogarth Press and The Institute of Psycho-Analysis; 1953).

————. 'Remembering, Repeating and Working-Through (Further Recommendations on the Technique of Psychoanalysis),' in *The Standard Edition of the Complete Psychological Works of Sigmund Freud*, vol. XII, edited and translated by J. Strachey and A. Freud (London, 1962 [1914], 144–56). See also Freud, Sigmund. 'Erinnern, Wiederholen und Durcharbeiten,' in Gesammelte Werke, vol. X (Frankfurt, 1999 [1914], 126–36).

————. 'Fragment of an Analysis of a Case of Hysteria' (1905[1901], p12), in *The Standard Edition of the Complete Psychological Works of Sigmund Freud*, vol. VII, (1901–1905): *A Case of Hysteria, Three Essays on Sexuality, and Other Works*, edited and translated by J. Strachey and A. Freud (London: The Hogarth Press and The Institute of Psycho-Analysis; 1953).

Gillberg, Asa and Jensen, Ola W. 'Processes of professionalization and marginalization – a constructivist study of archaeological field practices in Sweden 1870–1910,' in *Arkeologins många roller och praktiker: två sessioner vid VIII Nordic TAG i Lund*; 2005 (April 20–23; Lund, Sweden. Lund: Lund University, Department of Archaeology and Ancient History, 2007, 9–32 [Archaeology @ Lund, vol. 1]).

Gowland, William. 'The Recent Excavations at Stonehenge, with Inferences as to the Origin, Construction, and Purpose of That Monument,' *Man* 2 (1902, 7–11).

———. 'Recent Excavations at Stonehenge,' *Archaeologia* 58 (1902, 37–105).

Green, Miranda J. *Exploring the World of the Druids* (London, Thames and Hudson, 1997).

Greene, Kevin. *Archaeology: An Introduction*, fourth edition (London, Routledge, 2002).

Grinker, Roy Richard. *Fifty Years in Psychiatry: A Living History* (Springfield, IL, Charles C. Thomas Publisher Ltd, 1979).

Hawkins, Gerald S. 'Stonehenge Decoded,' *Nature* 200 (1963, 306–8).

———. 'Stonehenge: A Neolithic Computer,' *Nature* 202 (1964, 1258–61).

———. *Stonehenge Decoded* (London, Fontana/Collins, 1965).

Hellberg, Thomas and Lars Magnus Jansson. *Alfred Nobel* (Karlshamn, Lagerblads Förlag AB, 1986).

Hill, Rosemary. *Stonehenge* (London, Profile, 2008).

Huntington, Patricia A. M. 'Robert E. Peary and the Cape York Meteorites,' *Polar Geography* 26 (2002, 53–65).

Isaacson, Walter. *Einstein: His Life and Universe* (New York, Simon & Schuster, 2007).

Johnstone, Paul. *The Sea-craft of Prehistory* (London, Routledge & Kegan Paul, 1980).

Jung, Carl. *The Collected Works of C. G. Jung*, edited by H. Read, M. Fordham and G. Adler (London, Routledge, 1953).

Kandel, Eric R. 'Biology and the future of psychoanalysis: a new intellectual framework for psychiatry revisited' *American Journal of Psychiatry* 156 (1999, 505–24).

Karlinsky, Harry. *The Evolution of Inanimate Objects: The Life and Collected Works of Thomas Darwin 1857–1879* (London, HarperCollins, 2012).

Kipling, Rudyard. *Puck of Pook's Hill* (New York, Doubleday, Page & Company, 1906).

———. *Rudyard Kipling's verse: inclusive edition, 1885-1918* (New York, Doubleday, Page & Co., 1919).

———. 'o Beloved Kids': *Rudyard Kipling's Letters to His Children*, edited by Elliot L. Gilbert (San Diego, Harcourt, 1984).

———. *Something of Myself and Other Autobiographical Writings*, edited by Thomas Pinney (Cambridge, Cambridge University Press, 1990).

———. *The Letters of Rudyard Kipling Volume 3: 1900–1910*, edited by Thomas Pinney (London, Macmillan Press, 1996).

Klindt-Jensen, Ole. *A History of Scandinavian Archaeology*, translated by G. Russell Poole (London, Thames and Hudson, 1975).

Kramer, Peter D. *Freud: Inventor of the Modern Mind* (New York, Harper-Collins, 2006).

Larsson, Ulf. *Alfred Nobel: Networks of Innovation* (Stockholm, Nobel Museum, 2008).

Larsson, Ulf (editor). *Cultures of Creativity: The Centennial Exhibition of the Nobel Prize* (Canton, MA, Science History Publications, 2001).

Lehrer, Jonah. *Proust Was a Neuroscientist* (New York, Houghton Mifflin Company, 2007).

Lockyer, Norman. 'An Attempt to Ascertain the Date of the Original Construction of Stonehenge from its Orientation,' *Proceedings of the Royal Society* 69 (1901, 137–47).

———. *Stonehenge and Other British Stone Monuments Astronomically Considered* (London, Macmillan, 1906).

Lockyer, Norman and W. Rutherford. *The Rules of Golf* (London, Macmillan & Co., 1896).

Lycett, Andrew. *Rudyard Kipling* (London, Weidenfeld & Nicolson, 1999).

Macdonald, Meryl. *The Long Trail: Kipling Round the World* (Bristol, Tideway House, 1999).

Maugham, Andrew. 'Buried Alive: The Gothic Awakening of Taphephobia,' *Journal of Literature and Science* 3 (2010, 10–22).

Montelius, Oscar. *Remains from the Iron Age of Scandinavia* (Stockholm, Haggström, 1869).

Moore, Henry. *Stonehenge* (London, Ganymed, 1974).

Nicolson, Adam. *The Hated Wife: Carrie Kipling, 1862–1939* (London, Short Books, 2001).

Nobelprize.org. (Nobel Media AB, 2013).

Parker Pearson, Mike. *Stonehenge: Exploring the Greatest Stone Age Mystery* (London, Simon & Schuster Ltd, 2012).

Peary, Robert E. Northward Over the 'Great Ice.' *A Narrative of Life and Work Along the Shores and Upon the Interior Ice-cap of Northern Greenland in the Years 1886 and 1891–1897*, 2 vols. (London, Methuen & Co., 1898).

Quinn, Susan. *Marie Curie: A Life* (New York, Simon & Schuster, 1995).

Richards, Julian. *Stonehenge* (London, English Heritage Guidebook, 2011).

Roazen, Paul. 'Freud's Last Will,' *Journal of the American Academy of Psychoanalysis* 18 (1990, 383–85).

Roosevelt, Theodore. *The Autobiography of Theodore Roosevelt* (New York, The Macmillan Company, 1913).

———. *African Game Trails, the Account of the African Wanderings of an American Hunter–Naturalist* (New York, Scribner, 1919).

Roth, Nathan. *The Psychiatry of Writing a Will* (Springfield, IL, Charles C. Thomas, 1989).

Rubenfeld, Jed. *The Interpretation of Murder* (New York, Henry Holt and Company, 2006).

Sachs, Hanns. *Freud: Master and Friend* (Cambridge, MA., Harvard University Press, 1944).

Schück, Henrik et al., *Nobel – The Man and His Prizes*, edited by the Nobel Foundation Stockholm (Norman, OK, University of Oklahoma Press, 1951).

Sjöman, Vilgot (translated from the German by Karen Nyman). *Mitt hjärtebarn: de länge hemlighållna breven mellan Alfred Nobel och hans älskarinna Sofie* (Stockholm, Natur och kultur, 1995).

Soderland, Ulrica. *The Nobel Banquets: A Century of Culinary History 1901–2001*, translated by Michael Knight (Singapore, World Scientific Publishing, 2005).

Sohlman, Ragnar. *Ett Testamente. Nobelstiftelsens tillkomsthistoria och dess grundare* (Stockholm, P.A. Norstedt & Söners Förlag, 1950). Translated as *The Legacy of Alfred Nobel: The Story Behind the Nobel Prizes* (London, The Bodley Head, 1983).

Stenersen, Øivin, Ivar Libæk and Asle Sveen. *The Nobel Peace Prize: One Hundred Years for Peace· Laureates 1901–2000* (Oslo, Cappelen, 2001).

Stolt, Carl-Magnus. 'Why did Freud Never Receive the Nobel Prize?,' *International Forum of Psychoanalysis* 10 (2001, 221–26).

———. 'Moniz, Lobotomy, and the 1949 Prize,' in *Historical Studies in the Nobel Archives: The Prizes in Science and Medicine*, edited by Elisabeth Crawford (Tokyo, Universal Academy Press, 2002, 79–93).

Tartakoff, Helen H. 'The Normal Personality in Our Culture and the Nobel Prize Complex,' in *Psychoanalysis – A General Psychology: Essays in Honor of Heinz Hartman*, edited by R. M. Lowenstein et al. (New York, International University Press, 1966, 222–52).

Thomas, Herbert H. 'The Source of the Stones of Stonehenge,' *Antiquaries Journal* 3 (1923, 239–60).

Todes, Daniel. *Ivan Pavlov: Exploring the Animal Machine* (Oxford, Oxford University Press, 2000).

Vonnegut, Kurt. *Timequake* (New York, Putnam, 1997).

Waddell, John. 'The Irish Sea in Prehistory,' *The Journal of Irish Archaeology* 6 (1993, 29–40).

Wells, H. G. 'Russia in the Shadow. Second Article: Drift and Salvage,' *New York Times* (Nov 14 1920).

Wheelis, Allen. 'The Place of Action in Personality Change,' *Psychiatry* 13 (1950, 135–48).

Whitrow, Magda. 'Wagner-Jauregg and Fever Therapy,' *Medical History* 34 (1990, 294–310).

Wilkinson, Alec. 'The Ice Balloon,' *The New Yorker* 86 (2010, 38–46).

ILLUSTRATION CREDITS

Every effort has been made by the author to credit organizations and individuals with regard to the supply of photographs. Please notify the publishers regarding corrections.

Frontispiece: Trilithons B and C from the south-west, Stonehenge, c. 1867, Ordnance Survey. © The British Library Board.

Fig. 1: Nemon's bust of Freud. Freud Museum London.

Fig. 2: The Nobel Family. Immanuel Nobel (top left), Andriette Nobel (top right), and the Nobel brothers: Robert, Alfred, Ludvig, and baby Emil (bottom, clockwise from top). All photographs © The Nobel Foundation.

Fig. 3: Alfred Nobel. Photograph © The Nobel Foundation.

Fig. 4: Rudolf Lilljeqvist. Photographer Leverin, Stockholm. National Library of Sweden [KB KoB Lilljeqvist, Rudolf Fa1].

Fig. 5: The one-legged stool. Photograph © The Nobel Foundation.

Fig. 6: Ragnar Sohlman. Photographer Leverin, Stockholm. National Library of Sweden [KB KoB Sohlman, Ragnar Fa1].

Fig. 7: Two photographs of S. A. Andrée's Arctic balloon expedition in 1897. Library of Congress, Prints & Photographs Division, [LC-USZ61-1740].

Fig. 8: The first page of Alfred Nobel's will. Photograph © The Nobel Foundation.

Fig. 9: Sofie Hess. Photographer Krzinanek, Wien. National Library of Sweden [MS Acc 2007/9 Nobel: 6].

Fig. 10: Bertha von Suttner. Photograph © The Nobel Foundation.

Fig. 11: Stonehenge. Photograph by Miss Clarisse Miles. Adapted by Catherine MacDonald.

Fig. 12: Florence Antrobus. The Lady Antrobus House Charitable Trust, Amesbury.

Fig. 13: Carl Lindhagen. National Library of Sweden [Lindhagen, Carl Sv.P. 1].

Fig. 14: Oscar Montelius. Oscar Montelius Private Archive, the Antiquarian–Topographical Archive, the Swedish National Heritage Board, Sweden.

Fig. 15: A Sentimental and Practical Guide to Stonehenge, by Lady Antrobus. Adaptation and photography by Catherine MacDonald.

Fig. 16: The Lithology of Stonehenge. As found in *A Sentimental and Practical Guide to Amesbury and Stonehenge*, compiled by Lady Antrobus. Adapted by Catherine MacDonald.

Fig. 17 A Great Trilithon (top), Stonehenge (bottom). Photographs by Miss Clarisse Miles.

Fig. 18 Ivan Pavlov. U.S. National Library of Medicine.

Fig. 19 Rudyard Kipling. George Grantham Bain Collection, Library of Congress, Prints & Photographs Division [LC-DIG-ggbain-03724].

Fig. 20 Theodore Roosevelt, standing next to dead elephant, holding gun. Photographer Edward Van Altena. Library of Congress, Prints & Photographs Division [LC-USZ62-131443].

Fig. 21 Portrait of Robert Peary in furs, 1909, photogravure. Photographer Benjamin B. Hampton. Public Domain, Wikimedia Commons.

Fig. 22 Marie Curie. U.S. National Library of Medicine.

Fig. 23 Grand Hôtel, Stockholm. Courtesy of Grand Hôtel, Stockholm.

Fig. 24 1901 Banquet Menu. Adapted by Catherine MacDonald (utilising details from Soderland, U. The Nobel Banquets).

Fig. 25 Albert Einstein. Photographer Harris & Ewing. Library of Congress, Prints & Photographs Division [LC-H27-A-2848].

Fig. 26 Stonehenge. Photograph by Miss Clarisse Miles. Adapted by Catherine MacDonald.

Fig. 27 Details of a rather indistinct Early Bronze Age hilted dagger and several flat axes pecked into stone 53. The graffiti of later generations is also visible. Photographer R. J. C. Atkinson. © English Heritage.

Fig. 28 Sigmund Freud. Photographer John Carl Flugel or Ingeborg Flugel. Library of Congress, Prints & Photographs Division [LC-USZ62-119775].

Unnumbered Illustrations

p. 116 Section through one of the fallen Druidical stones at Stonehenge – This image is Fig. 7 in Darwin, C. *The Formation of Vegetable Mould, Through the Action of Worms, with Observations on Their Habits.* Reproduced by kind permission of the Syndics of Cambridge University Library.

p. 117 Pot of earthworms. Original drawing by Catherine MacDonald.

p. 118 Dissected earthworm. Adaptation and drawing by Catherine MacDonald (inspired by the work of Charles Darwin).

p. 124 From Bateman's to Stonehenge. Original drawing by Catherine MacDonald (inspired by Rudyard Kipling's drawings).

p. 130 Puck. Adaptation and drawing by Catherine MacDonald (inspired by the work of Harold Robert Millar).

p. 143 From Mt. Killaraus to Stonehenge. Original drawing by Catherine MacDonald.

p. 155 Curve of Knowns. Adaptation and drawing by Catherine MacDonald (utilizing details from Arnold, J. R. and W. F. Libby. 'Age Determinations by Radiocarbon Content: Checks with Samples of Known Age').

p. 163 Stonehenge: 1680 BC. Adaptation and drawing by Catherine MacDonald (utilizing details from Albrecht. 'Das Großsteindenkmal Avebury in Südengland').

p. 210 Florence Antrobus. Photographer Thomas Lionel Fuller. Courtesy of Jim Fuller.

p. 211 Marie Curie. Getty Images, Hulton Archive.

p. 211 Albert Einstein. Photographer Orren Jack Turner, c. 1947. Library of Congress, Prints & Photographs Division [LC-USZ62-60242].

p. 212 Sigmund Freud. Freud Museum London.

p. 213 Sofie Hess. Photographer C. Neumann, Wien. Private collection, Vienna. Copy: National Library of Sweden [MS Acc 2007/9 Nobel:6].

p. 214 Rudyard Kipling. Library of Congress, Prints & Photographs Division [LC-USZ62-12229].

p. 215 Rudolf Lilljeqvist. Courtesy of Anne-Charlotte and Jonas Lilljeqvist.

p. 216 Carl Lindhagen. Public Domain, Wikimedia Commons.

p. 216 Norman Lockyer. Courtesy of Special Collections, University of Exeter.

p. 217 Oscar Montelius. Photograph courtesy of Antiquarian–Topographical Archives, the National Heritage Board, Stockholm.

p. 218 Alfred Nobel. Photograph © The Nobel Foundation.

p. 219 Ivan Pavlov. Library of Congress, Prints & Photographs Division [LC-USZ62-117329].

p. 220 Theodore Roosevelt. Photographer Harris & Ewing. Library of Congress, Prints & Photographs Division [LC-DIG-hec-15042].

p. 21 Ragnar Sohlman. National Library of Sweden [KB KoB Sohlman, Ragnar AB].

p. 221 Bertha von Suttner. Library of Congress, Prints & Photographs Division [LC-USZ62-107347].

Harry Karlinsky obtained his medical degree from the University of Manitoba, his specialty degree in psychiatry from the University of Toronto and his Masters in Neuroscience degree from the University of London, England. An alumnus of Simon Fraser University's The Writer's Studio, he is currently a clinical professor of psychiatry at the University of British Columbia. His first novel, *The Evolution of Inanimate Objects The Life and Collected Works of Thomas Darwin (1857–1879)*, was shortlisted for the Wellcome Trust Book Prize.

Typeset in Adobe Caslon Pro
Printed at the Coach House on bpNichol Lane in Toronto, Ontario, on Rolland Opaque Natural paper, which was manufactured, acid-free, in Saint-Jérôme, Quebec, from 50 percent recycled paper, and it was printed with vegetable-based ink on a 1965 Heidelberg KORD offset litho press. Its pages were folded on a Baumfolder, gathered by hand, bound on a Sulby Auto-Minabinda and trimmed on a Polar single-knife cutter.

Edited by Scott Pack and Alana Wilcox
Designed by Alana Wilcox
Cover photo by Ifan Bates

Coach House Books
80 bpNichol Lane
Toronto ON M5S 3J4
Canada

416 979 2217
800 367 6360

mail@chbooks.com
www.chbooks.com